MW01146351

The Opiate

Your literary dose.

© The Opiate 2024
Cover art: Publicity photo of Jean Harlow for Metro-Goldwyn-Mayer circa the 1930s.
This magazine, or parts thereof, may not be reproduced without permission.
Contact theopiatemagazine@gmail.com for queries.

"All she wanted was to be a little girl, to be efficiently taken care of by some yielding yet superior power, stupider and steadier than herself. It seemed that the only lover she had ever wanted was a lover in a dream."
-F. Scott Fitzgerald

"I am too intelligent, too demanding, and too resourceful for anyone to be able to take charge of me entirely. No one knows me or loves me completely. I have only myself."
-Simone de Beauvoir

Editor-in-Chief
Genna Rivieccio

Editor-at-Large
Malik Crumpler

Editorial Advisor
Anton Bonnici

Contributing Writers:

Fiction:

Poetry:

Criticism:

Editor's Note

The dichotomy of what it "means" to be a woman only seems to be intensifying all the more in the twenty-first century. With each passing year that women are hurtled into the alleged future, it doesn't feel as though it's getting any easier to define our "place" in this still male-dominated world. *Especially* politically. Although this issue will come out before knowing the results of the U.S. presidential election, a win for Kamala Harris doesn't necessarily signal the change that so many (women and men alike) are hoping for. In fact, there's plenty of reason to believe that, (Indian and Black) woman or not, Harris will remain nothing more than a government puppet (and, as such, continue to funnel millions of dollars into providing weapons to Israel, the most "Western" country in the Middle East). Just another face that will serve only as a front for what's really going on behind the scenes.

Indeed, one of the main reasons (apart from white supremacy) that people still have the audacity to declare their "preference" for Trump is that he "dares" to "tell the truth" a.k.a. be on blast about his corruption. Some, apparently, see that as "refreshing"—a roundabout form of "honesty." At least in this Black Lodge world where everything—including logic—has been twisted and tainted into some perverse "alternate form." This extends, again, to the dichotomy of how women are supposed to be defined in a world that still demands that they exist in a convenient little box that itself fits neatly within patriarchal boundaries. That women are inherently more three-dimensional than men only further adds to the irony of this expectation. Not to mention the sheer impossibility of it.

Even so, women still try at being as two-dimensional as they can in order to accommodate a world that effectively insists upon it. This is part of the reason why Harris has been so blatantly shat upon throughout the election for her "dual" identity: being both Indian and Black. It is the latter part of herself that people—Trump (himself orange) included—have not only taken the most issue with, but have also tried to use as a means to discredit her (and, needless to say, there are far more viable things to discredit her for). As though she's somehow "lying" about who she is for so-called clout.

And this is precisely what Trump accused her of as he insinuated (with all the subtlety of an anvil) that she "became" Black for the purpose of catering to the "correct" sect of identity politics. The quintessentially grotesque and crude manner in which he chose to tout that opinion occurred at, of all venues, a convention for the National Association of Black Journalists as he deviated (*quelle surprise*) from the question at hand to say, "[Kamala] was always of Indian heritage. She was only promoting Indian heritage. I didn't know she was Black until a number of years ago when she happened to turn *Black*. And now she wants to be known as *Black*. So I don't know, is she Indian or is she Black?" Here, too, Trump highlights the general partiarchal inability to compute that a woman can be more than one thing, instead insisting that she must be "either/or"— virgin *or* whore, pretty *or* smart, careerist *or* mother and, now, evidently, Indian *or* Black. But never *both*. Never *two* things at once, let alone *multiple* things at once. Heaven forbid a man could "let" a woman be anything more complex. "Let" her tick off more than one box on the metaphorical census form.

In the same interview, Trump then continued to racistly and misogynistically drone on, "I respect either one, but she obviously doesn't. Because she was Indian all the way and then all of the sudden she made a turn and she went, she became a Black person." First of all, one doesn't "choose" a race, itself yet another social construct. But of course, Trump is suggesting that it suddenly became more politically conducive to play up what he falsely bills as a nonexistent aspect of her identity.

Worse still, one of Harris' theoretical own, Janet Jackson, echoed that sentiment months later in a now notorious interview with *The Guardian* during which she cavalierly stated, "She's not Black. That's what I heard. That she's Indian." The interviewer then interjects, "She looks at me expectantly, perhaps assuming I have Indian heritage. 'Well, she's both,' I offer." Jackson added, "'Her father's white. That's what I was told. I mean, I haven't watched the news in a few days,' she coughs. 'I was told that they discovered her father was white.'" The journalist, Nosheen Iqbal, then writes, "I'm floored at this point. It's well known that Harris' father is a Jamaican economist, a Stanford professor who split from her Indian mother when she was five. 'My mother understood very well that she was raising two Black daughters,' Harris wrote in her book, *The Truths We Hold*. The people who are most vocal in questioning the facts of Harris' identity tend to be hardcore QAnon-adjacent, Trump-loving conspiracy theorists." But Jackson being, as far as anyone knows, neither of those things, well, it just plays into the fact that people who question the "validity" of Harris' identity aren't "extreme," so much as intrinsically conditioned by society to believe that women do not contain multitudes (with women themselves [e.g., Jackson] often being even guiltier of possessing this belief than their opposite).

That, in the end, remains an ostensible "divine right" of men. And, as mentioned, such a luxury is wasted on them in that the only multitudes they contain tend to exist within the plentiful ways in which they delight in torturing and discriminating against women.

A fragile little girl/diabolical demon (though surely not both at the same time!),

Genna Rivieccio
October 2024

P.S. For those "offended" enough to want to employ the "not all men" defense, refer, then, to Joanna Russ' sarcastic quote from *On Strike Against God* to soothe yourselves: "...not all men make more money than all women, only most; that not all men are rapists, only some; that not all men are promiscuous killers, only some; that not all men control Congress, the Presidency, the police, the army, industry, agriculture, law, science, medicine, architecture and local government, only some."

FICTION

A Good Night For The Other

Charles Wilkinson

"I waved but you didn't see me."

The man speaking to Henry Case is dressed in a black t-shirt and dark tracksuit bottoms so baggy as to be Chaplin-esque. He has thin white arms with tattoos designed for a much larger man—if he were to be blown up like a plastic doll, they would expand to become as recognizable as body art. As it is, they are barely legible, a bubonic purple and black.

"It's Tosh."

"In what way?"

"No, that's my name. Tosh."

The fitness studio is full for a Friday evening. The P.E. teacher from the local comprehensive, her hair drawn back tight from her forehead, is pounding the treadmill. The *swish-swish* of the rowing machine competes with the Top Forty countdown playing on two televisions affixed to the oatmeal-colored walls. As always, the man in the yellow sweatshirt is lifting weights, raising them carefully to the light. There's something hieratic about his slow movements; the metal glints like a chalice. Although Henry's noticed Tosh before, he's never paid much attention to him until now.

"Hello, Tosh," he says neutrally. He is not disposed to reveal his name is Henry. By way of distraction, he adds, "I probably wasn't wearing my glasses. Pretty much everything in the middle distance and beyond is a blur without them."

Tosh's short, greasy hair has been dyed yellow-green, giving his roundish head the appearance of a damp tennis ball.

"Yeh, seen you in here, of course. And about. With your lady. Very nice-looking woman, she is. Your lady."

Henry nods at nowhere in particular and then gives a constricted smile before turning (though not so quickly as to be dismissive) towards the steps machine. Working on it will necessarily mean he has his back to Tosh.

Then the voice comes softly: "I wouldn't mind giving her a bit of the other."

***

His wife is slumped in an armchair in the sitting room. She's surrounded by cardboard boxes, one of which she uses as a footrest. Henry is not sure why it's taking them so long to finish unpacking. After all, it's been almost two months since they moved in. The television is off and her magazine remains unopened on the side table. With her luminously pale skin and long, golden hair, she's a lady in an Arthurian legend from the neck up. But the orange woolen jumper (which obscures the line of her breasts), the faded jeans and torn trainers could never have been rendered romantic, even by the Pre-Raphaelites.

"Paint," she says, as he watches him sit down in the other chair.

In the last week or so, she's become increasingly laconic. He decides not to ask her to expand. The word hovers between them, neither noun nor verb.

"I long for the smell of it," she adds, with feeling.

He has never seen her so angry and glum. For once, he decides to indulge her. "And why would that be?"

"Because then we would be in our own home. Decorating. Here, I hardly feel it was worth taking my underwear out of the suitcase. How much longer are we going to be in this fetid little town?"

"A minimum of four months...six at the very most."

He has started to turn the store around. Foot traffic is increasing every day and sales are up. Last month, they actually made a profit. But he won't be leaving until he's absolutely certain the business model is sustainable. Henry's appreciated at Head Office. In the last three years, he's revamped and revivified ten branches from Aberdeen to Saint Austell. Of course, it's meant living in rented accommodations. During the first year, his wife laughed whenever he claimed at dinner parties that such an existence was "good for our sense of geography."

"And so where will we be by next winter? Wales? Washington State? Let's try somewhere rainy. And as far as possible from our relatives or any friends we might have left."

The art of administration includes knowing when to ignore bitter irony and how to avoid responding to questions one has no intention of answering. Henry's been working on a surprise for some time. It's not a hundred percent ready, but right now he has need of it.

"A beach holiday—or a few weeks in the sun by a pool. That's what I think comes next."

"As if to emphasize her new-found lack of sobriety, she whips the cork out and fills her glass to the brim. Henry has learned that when someone is set on such a course of action, a display of disapproval is counterproductive; he must wait for an opportune moment to manage her behavior."

She takes her feet off the cardboard box and swivels towards him. "You haven't told me about this." Her eyes are brighter, as if she can already see the surf.

"I'm still negotiating with Humphrey Stapleton at Head Office. It's not absolutely certain, but we'll be able to go once I'm finished here. It's a promise. Of course, it's far too soon to book anything, but there's no harm in doing research if you want to."

Once she's on her laptop, he tells her he's going to take a shower. Halfway up the staircase, he stands to congratulate himself and offer thanks. He's in control again. And there *will* be a holiday. What his wife doesn't realize is that *he* wants one as well: it's a pact he's made with himself. He longs to watch sunlight falling on his son's brown back.

He edges past the packing cases on the landing and into the spare room he uses whenever he's been working late, which is often. Most of his possessions are in there. Opposite is the boy's bedroom. Either he's out or he's working quietly. Henry tells himself he's a man who deserves his luck: good health, a beautiful wife and son—along with all the benefits allied to being a perfect manager of people.

***

The fitness studio is so crowded that, at first, Henry doesn't spot Tosh.

The man in the yellow sweatshirt stands by the weights. He's the only person present who treats exercise as essentially meditative; his every movement is pondered. Sometimes, he sits for three or four minutes between lifts; at other moments, he circles the apparatus watchfully, as if waiting for a dumbbell to make the first move. A prim-lipped elderly man with granny glasses and thinning hair pedals sedately on an exercise bike. Henry's reminded of a previous prime minister's observation about old maids cycling to evensong being the essence of Englishness. Boys from the comprehensive are taking turns on the rowing machine. There's a group of women in their late thirties standing by the abdominal crunch; they talk in confidential tones and glance around to make sure no one's eavesdropping.

The door opens. For a second, they hear booming cries, the swimming pool wardens' echoing voices and the crash of diving from the high board. Henry has picked up an exercise mat and is trying to find a vacant spot when he sees Tosh leaning against the far wall. He has a towel over his shoulder and is drinking from his plastic water bottle. Their eyes meet before Henry strides off to his corner; in his peripheral vision, he's aware of Tosh waving for an instant.

Henry's out by the drink dispenser in the lobby when someone taps him on the shoulder. He doesn't turn around before collecting his apple juice and change. Tosh is standing at a distance that would be thought discourteous or worse had the machine been an ATM. What's odd is how Tosh has filled out since Henry saw him a fortnight ago. His shoulders are broader, and he appears less adrift in his baggy tracksuit bottoms. He's wearing a bright red baseball cap. As he lifts his water bottle to his lips, a previously slender bicep bulges. Has he been going to the gym every day?

"Good place this?" asks Tosh.

"In what respect?"

"Open to the general public for a couple of quid. Not private, like. Even let rubbish like me in. Eh, Henry! What do you think about that?"

Henry isn't going to ask him how he knows his name. Why shouldn't Tosh be aware of who he is? After all, Henry *is* the new manager of the largest business concern in town and has no doubt already sacked several of Tosh's unprepossessing associates.

"Good value is always to be applauded wherever it's offered."

"That so, Henry? And what about your missus? Your other half. Is she offering anything of 'good value' lately?"

Henry replies to this by stepping almost straight towards Tosh—not so close as to risk a collision, but just near enough to make him sway to one side. As he opens the door to the fitness studio, he hears Tosh call out, "'Round your place earlier, I was. Looking at a bit of the other! I'm waving again, Henry. Turn 'round and you'll see me!"

***

Outside, it is dusk and the street light near the bench is on, glossing the green metal with yellow. The beech trees' upper branches are blurred masses of dark foliage. It is easy to imagine a man with binoculars in the tree—stretched out, biding his time for a while on a bough, waiting for the windows in the street to light up, one by one. Henry draws the curtains close; there will not be a crack for approaching darkness to breach.

When he comes into the kitchen, he is surprised to see she has poured herself a glass of wine, which is something she does infrequently.

"Want to join me?" She gestures towards a bottle of red.

"Thank you. But not on a Tuesday."

As if to emphasize her newfound lack of sobriety, she whips the cork out and fills her glass to the brim. Henry has learned that when someone is set on such a course of action, a display of disapproval is counterproductive; he must wait for an opportune moment to manage her behavior.

"You didn't see anyone snooping around here earlier?"

"No. Why...should I have done?"

"A man in a red baseball cap."

She takes a sip of the wine. "I don't think so."

"Are you sure?"

A pause while she contemplates the level in the bottle. "There might have been someone sitting on the bench. I don't think he was wearing a baseball cap."

"What did he look like?"

"I really can't remember. Does it matter? All I want to know is when we're going to leave this place."

There have been other small towns she's taken a dislike to, but this is the first place where she's made no effort whatsoever to find new acquaintances. As a top-rate businessman, Henry is always careful to make no close friends, but his wife usually craves a social life to sustain her, even if it revolves around charity work.

"If you do see anyone suspicious there when I'm out, phone me at the office."

"For heaven's sake, Henry. All sorts of people sit on that bench. I very much doubt if any of them have the slightest interest in us."

He will not deign to argue with her while she is drinking. As it happens, there is another matter he intends to raise with her. His wife has moved several of the packing cases into the boy's room, even though he asked her not to. It's simply unfair to his son.

"We'll discuss this another time."

He goes upstairs and carries the cardboard boxes out onto the landing. As a concession to her complaints, he stacks them one on top of the other. Then he peers back into the room. It's not as tidy as he would have liked, but at least there's now plenty of space.

***

Tosh appears next to Henry just as he's rinsing his soapy hands in the bathroom. Next to them the urinal hisses; the sound mingles with a cistern's music of water and metal clanking. Tosh turns on the faucet, but makes no attempt to wash. Henry pulls out the stopper in his basin: a gurgling followed by a swallow; then the final gulp.

"Good session, Henry?"

"Perfectly satisfactory."

"Hope you don't mind me following you in here. But I fancy a word...in private. There's no one on the bog is there?"

"Not so far as I am aware."

"It's about your missus. And I don't want you to take offense, Henry. But I think she's not getting it: a bit of the other. I'm not saying that she's not getting enough of it. I don't think she's getting it at all."

Even though his hands are wet, Henry makes no movement towards the towels. Now that he studies Tosh more closely, assesses him for the first time in a week, he is amazed to see how much muscle the man has put on in what must be only a matter of a month or so. Has this been achieved without chemical assistance? The man's head is quite small; in comparison to his wide shoulders and powerful fore-arms, it appears almost decorative. His tattoos have expanded to become two scrolled expletives.

"I can't think what you're driving at."

"Is that right? I'm saying there's a lovely lady that needs seeing to, mate. But I'll tell you this: next time I see you, if I've done your missus good and proper, I'll give you a little wave." Tosh demonstrates the little wave as he makes his way to the door.

In the lobby, Henry is in time to see Tosh push through the double doors leading to the path onto the main road. A group of primary school children with wet hair and towels furled like Arctic rolls have surrounded the drinks dispenser. The man behind the reception desk studies a computer screen and strokes his stubble. In the swimming pool area, wardens in Aertex shirts and blue shorts use poles to retrieve abandoned Lilos, bodyboards and brightly colored balls, several of which have floated tantalizingly out of reach. Instead of leaving, as he'd intended, Henry decides to return to the fitness studio. The man in the yellow sweatshirt is working on the parallel bars, his mulberry face contorting and grimacing. The muscles on his upper body are grotesquely well-developed in contrast to his spindly white legs. Once he's finished and is busy wiping himself down, Henry walks over to him.

"That chap Tosh who was in here earlier...do you know him?"

"Lots of men come in here."

"He sometimes wears a red baseball cap."

"What's it to you?" The man looks at Henry for the first time. His small black eyes flicker with inexplicable anger.

"He's engaged me in conversation on a number of occasions. I simply wish to know more about him." Henry's aware of sounding a tad orotund; his vowel sounds too full for the occasion.

The man unzips his carrier bag violently and thrusts his towel and trainers inside. Then he stands almost upright, his head jutting forward. Although his hands are on his hips, it seems perfectly possible that, at any second, he will grip Henry by the throat.

"Listen, I don't want anyone 'engaging' *me*. Got that?!" He picks up his carrier bag as if yanking someone upright by the hair.

Once the man in the yellow sweatshirt has seethed off into the lobby, Henry is alone in the fitness studio for the first time. The sound on the television has been turned off; the unaccompanied, onscreen gyrations of the exotic dancers are neither primitive nor sensual, but peculiarly meaningless. Henry climbs onto the nearest exercise bike and begins to pedal. He, too, is beginning to dislike the small town, where a clear-cut inquiry can provoke a display of unprovoked aggression. Some of its inhabitants are beyond even *his* management skills. The screen lights up and Henry selects intermediate aerobics. He has lost weight and now has no fear of looking flabby on the beach. The boy should have a father he can be proud of, not some slob who disguises his paunch with an oversized short-sleeved shirt sporting a garish design of palm trees and parrots. He makes a conscious effort to set the incident with that barbarian of a bodybuilder to one side. Gradually, the tick of the spinning wheels induces a faint euphoria, the sense of

"It's about your missus. And I don't want you to take offense, Henry. But I think she's not getting it: a bit of the other. I'm not saying that she's not getting enough of it. I don't think she's getting it at all."

effortless progression that comes with being so much fitter. He leans forward and pedals faster. It's when he's halfway through the program that the noise suddenly increases. The ticking is counterpointed by a mysterious clicking that comes at regular intervals; the swishing now louder, yet less rhythmic. It's almost as if another rider has joined him. He glances to his left. The wheels on the exercise bike closest to him are turning, although there is no one on the saddle.

***

When confronted by phenomena or circumstances that appear beyond one's control, it is important to make a list. Henry is sitting at the kitchen table and studying the columns into which he has organized everything causing him concern. Problems with his leisure and home life outweigh his difficulties at work. Under the header "Solutions," the spaces linked to business have been filled in; the others are blank.

"So you haven't seen him? The man in the baseball cap?"

"No," his wife replies as she takes the lid off the slow cooker and inspects the contents.

Henry's ballpoint hovers over the column labeled "Stalker." Perhaps he is wrong to surmise Tosh is the man on the bench.

"Are you really going to the gym later? It's not one of your usual times."

"I've stopped going on Fridays. It's always overcrowded and seems to attract rather a strange clientele."

"Will you be late?"

"Not especially."

"I won't be going to bed early tonight, so there's no need for you to sleep in the spare room."

He picks up a ruler and carefully underlines the word "boy" in red ink. The space next to "child" is empty. There is an unbroken silence—apart from the clink of a ladle on the inside of the pot. Then he coughs and says, "I'm perfectly happy in the spare room."

"I know. That's what worries me. Developed an aversion to double beds, have you?"

He writes "demands for" next to "child."

"Soon it'll be too late. You know I want one," she adds, trying to keep a catch out of her voice.

"Don't you think we should wait until we're more settled? It would be very unfair to the boy...or girl...to keep changing schools."

She's heard this piece of prevarication so many times that she refuses to give it even a terse reply. Instead, she spoons the stew onto a plate and puts it out of easy reach on the table. If he says one more thing, she will suggest he should visit the doctor. He says it; she tells him.

After the argument, she phones her father.

Once he's finished his meal, he bolts for the stairs. Before going into the spare room to change, he stops outside the boy's door. He hears the faint hiss of headphones, the tap on the keyboard. But when he turns the handle and steps in, the room is silent—unfilled, as always. He allows his imagination to put up pictures of a favorite premier football team, some posters of a band. Under the window, he inserts a desk, and on it a lamp and a computer. A bed with a colorful counterpane. There's one bookcase; the top shelf is filled with adventures and tales of detection. A cricket bat, kissed with red on the sweet spot, leans against the corner. There's a tennis racket in the wardrobe. On afternoons when the boy is visible, staring out the window with his back to his father, he's slim with soft, brown hair; in winter, he wears a fleece with broad gray and salmon pink stripes. Henry has never seen his face.

***

He cannot accept that she is leaving. Later he will regain control. In the meantime, the only remedy for pain and panic is exercise. He is holding a plastic bag that contains his trainers and towel. He dislikes meeting anyone he knows when he is wearing a tracksuit, but the street is quiet, apart from the one shopkeeper who stayed open late and is carrying a blackboard inside. The pubs have opened their doors; the wine bar's windows are brassy with welcoming light. As Henry draws level with the frontage, he spots someone standing at the top of the steps. A baseball hat with a long peak obscures the top of the man's face, but the shoulders, broader than ever, are familiar. Henry tells himself to look away—at once. But before he can do so, the man waves, as if he's the captain of a winning team on an open-top bus tour of the town, and then leans towards him.

"Looks as if it's going to be a good night for the other. For both us...eh, Henry?"

At least Tosh won't be in the gym—a consolation of sorts. Henry quickens his pace. The way to manage such comedians is to refuse to respond to being goaded, then to retaliate at a time of one's choosing.

Early evening. The red brick façades in the High Street lose their traces of orange and darken to dried blood. To the west, pale powder clouds dissolve to streaky pinks; streamers ignite on the horizon. There's no one outside by the time Henry arrives; it's brown dusk—the buildings around the Leisure Centre have receded into the fur and pelt of shadow, lending the floodlit building architectural allure. He's glad the youths who loiter by the entrance smoking are not in evidence; beyond the double door, the lobby lights are on.

No one at the front desk, which is unusual. Henry peers into the fitness studio: not a single person. The treadmill's at rest; the wheels of the exercise bicycles are motionless; even the television screens are gunmetal rectangles. He steps back into the lobby. Something is missing; the drinks dispenser has vanished. If he wants to use the fitness studio, he must pay one of the attendants. The tiny office behind the reception desk has every appearance of being locked. He listens for soft explosions of diving, the splashes and echoing cries of children. The silence is filled by a low electrical hum. Nonetheless, he walks towards the swimming pool area and peers through the glass doors. The surface of the water is undisturbed. There are no wardens or bathers, although the lights are on.

In the circumstances, it's surely ethical to begin his routine in the fitness studio and pay once the reception desk is manned. But as he walks back into the lobby, he realizes it's dark beyond the double doors: the floodlights have been turned off. The galleries from which the spectators watch squash are on the upper story of the building, along with several storage cupboards. Perhaps an attendant is there. As Henry makes his way up the stairs, he hears the squeak, slap and squeal of trainers on the court, the *pock-pick* of the ball's variable resonance on the walls. Something about the rhythm of play suggests a coaching session rather than a match, or perhaps a father teaching his son. As soon as he reaches the corridor, he makes his way to the viewing gallery. There's no one on the court; the sounds continue. Cold incredulity crawls up his spine, converts to shock. Then the relief of explanation: it's quite simple—the noises are coming from the next-door court. Since there are no attendants in the gallery or corridor, he might as well go back down. The changing rooms are on the lower level; surely it's possible someone's tidying up in there. As he reaches the bottom of the stairs, he remembers: the Leisure Centre has only one squash court. He dashes to the double doors, but they're locked. Not an inch of the outside world is visible. It's as if someone has rolled up the path and taken it away into the night. A faint noise is coming from the swimming pool: a lapping of water against edges, the steady swish of a slow crawl; the susurration that comes with legs pushed against the edge when a swimmer turns. He wheels round. The light coming from the pool area is intense. As soon as he pushes the doors open, the water's a different color—a holiday aquamarine. A white bird soars upwards and melds with sunlight. The roof has disappeared. There is a faint splash from the middle of the pool; a slender arm rises—and vanishes.

Seconds later, he sees a figure idling near the bottom, the limbs slightly deformed by the trickery of depth. Slowly the swimmer rises, almost to the air, and then dives, as though to avoid being caught in the surface's quicksilver net. Henry peers down. Nothing—as if the swimmer has dissolved rather than drowned. Then sparkling wet hands on the pool's edge followed by a wet cap of dark brown hair; the face screwed up, the sunburned shoulders glistening. The boy blows out water, and blinks his eyes open. He is so like his father at the same age. Henry understands that if he takes a step forward, the pool's floor will change, shelf to shingle. He will find himself wading deeper, till his feet touch ribs of sand. Living below the breakers, as submarine as coral, the seahorse and the brittle star, he will know only the management of currents, each tide's control, the midnight moon's laws. He tries to take a step back, yet already the palm trees have grown tall. There are places that are more than anyone could promise; holidays from which it is impossible to return. The boy raises himself up onto a rock; he is half out of the boundless ocean, smiling with infinite, dark joy: "Come

> **"He cannot accept that she is leaving. Later he will regain control. In the meantime, the only remedy for pain and panic is exercise. He is holding a plastic bag that contains his trainers and towel. He dislikes meeting anyone he knows when he is wearing a tracksuit, but the street is quiet..."**

on, Dad! It's warm in here!"

***

Her father is upstairs dealing with Henry's possessions. It hasn't taken her long to get ready. She was free to leave, the police said. There were unlikely to be any further developments in the case now that the men in the town who'd been known to wear a red baseball cap had been interviewed. All were elsewhere at the estimated time of death. What remains a mystery is how Henry entered the Leisure Centre when it was locked on a Bank Holiday Monday.

"He's kept an extraordinary amount of stuff from his school days," her father shouts down to her. "Old football annuals, model cars. I shouldn't think his sister would want any of it."

"I hadn't realized he was such a hoarder."

"I'd better pack it up. Leave her to decide."

She wanders over to the front window and stares out at the crescent: the almost identical houses, distinguishable by the ornamental shrubs and dwarf conifers or the space given over to hard surfaces and

"Henry understands that if he takes a step forward, the pool's floor will change, shelf to shingle. He will find himself wading deeper, till his feet touch ribs of sand. Living below the breakers, as submarine as coral, the seahorse and the brittle star, he will know only the management of currents, each tide's control, the midnight moon's laws."

crazy paving. An elderly man on the bench is reading a newspaper. In a month or two, she tells herself, she will find it almost impossible to believe she has lived here. The view from this window will be no more than an image from a scene in a TV series she's almost forgotten. Since she has been in this place, it's as if she's been living without a name. Next time she will make her own decisions, ensure she dwells within the dignity of proper nouns.

"I think we're almost ready for the off now." She hears her father coming down the stairs.

She locks the front door. Once they're in the car and moving away from the town to which she will never return, she tries to explain to her father: "Henry was very strange recently. I think he thought I was having an affair. Perhaps because he refused to give me a child."

Henry was found in the swimming pool. Drowned but with no obvious signs of violence. She hadn't asked for any details, but in her dreams, he was poised between two elements, floating face down, open eyes staring through water, the back of his head and ballooning tracksuit top not quite submerged. The last time she saw him was just before she heard the front door bang as he set off to the gym. He was sitting at the kitchen table, his untouched meal out of reach. Whatever he'd been writing had vanished. For once, he was entirely still, his gaze fixed far beyond his surroundings, as if he were staring at the gap on the other side of his certainties.

Sea of Tranquility

Lance Romanoff

T he car, a shabby 1983 Saab 900, expired seven miles south of Eureka, Nevada. Finn and Saoirse O'Malley knew nothing about cars. They didn't even pump their own gas.

"I'll walk to the next town. It shouldn't be more than a few hours," Finn said.

"Right. And I'll sit here."

"I'm open to suggestions."

"I'm not comfortable sitting here alone for hours. Who knows who or *what* could show up?"

They sat, staring out the windshield at the unyielding road.

"Okay. I just thought I'd be saving you a long walk. There's no one out here. You're not in danger."

"*You* don't know what could happen. *I* don't know what could happen. You're insane if you think I'm just going to sit alone in a car in the middle of nowhere for hours."

"Fine. Okay. Fine. I'm not telling you *not* to come."

Saoirse folded down the passenger visor and stared into the scratched mirror. The mid-afternoon sun illuminated her white-blonde hair in a wild glow around her head.

Finn tightened his grip around the steering wheel. "It's just, there's no reason for both of us to go."

"There's no reason for *one* of us to stay."

A day before, they were happily gambling in Las Vegas. Saoirse won two hundred dollars playing blackjack. Finn played the slot machines and left the casino only a dollar richer.

"I'm not telling you to stay."

"Right, so...?"

"I'm just saying that it's going to be a long walk. You might as

"He discovered them, a gently crushed pack of Merits paired with a book of matches, in his inside pocket... 'Miracle in the desert,' Finn thought to himself as he lit one up."

well stay here and be comfortable at least. Nothing's going to happen."

"You don't know that."

"We're alone out here. If we weren't alone out here, I wouldn't have to walk! Jesus."

Finn tugged at his left eyebrow. It was a habit he acquired as a teenager to soothe his migraines. Now he pulled on his eyebrow whenever he wanted to say something, but thought better of it.

"There's no need for us to argue about this. I don't want to walk for several miles or however far it is either, but I'm not staying out here. And the longer we sit here and fight about it, the worse it will be."

"That much I agree with."

Neither moved. Finn sunk deeper into the driver's seat. He'd decided not to shave during their trip and now wore the early stages of a scratchy, graying beard.

Saoirse sighed. "This is what you do. You know this is what you do, don't you? You're turning this into a situation and making everything worse. You always do this."

"I 'always' do this? Every time we're stuck in the middle of nowhere, I do this?"

"You know what I'm talking about."

"I have no *fucking* idea what you're talking about."

"No, you probably don't."

Finn sucked in a long breath and opened his door. He took a leaden first step, and then a second and a third. A quarter mile down the road, he hunted around in his jacket for his cigarettes. He discovered them, a gently crushed pack of Merits paired with a book of matches, in his inside pocket. The matchbook was a glossy black and featured the Dunes Casino logo embossed across the cover.

"Miracle in the desert," Finn thought to himself as he lit one up.

He stared down the road in the direction of Eureka.

He thought about the six and a half miles left to walk.

He squinted at the horizon.

No town.

Turning back the way he came, he saw his wife sitting in the passenger seat of their car—staring at him, daring him to choose a direction.

"Are you coming?" Finn shouted, to no reply.

He marched back to the car and opened her door.

"Are you coming?" Finn asked again.

Saoirse turned to look at him, but said nothing.

"Are you coming?" Finn asked a third time.

"Just go if you want to go. I'll wait."

"Now you want to stay. Fine."

Finn dropped his cigarette and stamped it out into the earth. He stared at his wife. "Where did that two hundred dollars really come from?"

Saoirse studied his face. The features she'd known for years were now suddenly unfamiliar. "What are you talking about?"

"You don't know how to play blackjack. How do you win two hundred dollars when you're playing a game you don't know how to play?"

"Are you upset I won more than you? Is that seriously what we're talking about?"

"*Is* that what we're talking about?"

"I don't know. Tell me what we're talking about."

"I just don't understand how someone who doesn't play blackjack wins two hundred dollars at blackjack."

Saoirse stood up, pushing Finn aside as she rose.

She took a step toward the rear of the car.

Finn lit another cigarette. He dropped the flaming match at his feet and watched it burn itself out. "I just want to know where that money came from. I'm just asking where it came from."

"No. No. That's not what you're doing. You're doing what you do."

"What do I 'do'?"

"You're accusing me of something. Except you can't even do that. If you have something to say, just say it."

He stared at the burned match on the ground. "Miracle in the desert."

She noticed it first. Recognized it was a truck: maybe a box truck, or perhaps a tow. It seemed to squat there in the distance forever. Suddenly, the flat-fronted Ford resembling a hulking, mechanical bulldog choked to a stop with a squeal of air brakes.

Saoirse opened the passenger door and went over to speak with the driver. Finn watched her mouth move. He thought she might have smiled. But he heard nothing.

The Budding Telepathist Buys Fancy Enchiladas For His Wife

Daniel Allen Solomon

The guy at the enchilada store takes my order, and when I ask him if I should wait on the sidewalk by the other counter, he smiles at me. He says to me, "You got it, buddy."

That's the third time that he's called me "buddy," and it doesn't sound like it comes easy to him. It sounds like he's got to put a tiny bit of thought behind it to make it come out of his mouth, like he's just learned the word and he's overly eager to apply it to his speech.

I guess, to be honest, the big reason that "buddy" strikes me as weird is because he's a Latino dude, and I'm a white guy. Him calling me "buddy" from behind the cash register, and doing it repeatedly, feels to me like something in between unnecessary deference and...subtle mockery? I don't like it.

Maybe I'm being overanalytical, but let me give you some context. Number one piece of context is that this is Stanford Mall, which is, as you know, an upscale shopping center right by Stanford University in Stanford, California, in the USA. I can't afford to live within three miles of these enchiladas, but I'm here today, and often, because it's on the way home from work and I have developed the sick habit of exercising by jogging around the outstanding, idyllic suburbs of Stanford Hills, which is, for the record, someplace where I will never have any legitimate reason to be.

Number two piece of context is that I'm a little bit psychic. For instance, when the cashier called me "buddy" for the third time, I could hear echoes of some of the other times he had pronounced "buddy" across this counter to different people. A white man, an East Asian-derived person, a South Asian-derived person, a white and/or Asian-derived or mixed couple, a university student, a full-grown man in a hoodie and skinny jeans buying his enchilada with his phone app. Or to anyone just hanging out, wearing yoga pants and Gucci sunglasses, with a Louis Vuitton bag and a pug. I could hear the cashier saying to this person, "Hey buddy, I like your pug."

I have no confidence that I'm interpreting these echoes correctly. How should I know what anything means? But I get all that, and I still can't tell what the man's intention is.

Then I think, _Why wouldn't I want to be buds with him?_

And then I wonder, _Am I being racist again?_

Suddenly I'm embarrassed. Learning to wield my mental powers has been an interesting experience, not least because it's jacked up my anxiety. Now I _know_ that there are telepaths out there who are not revealing themselves to the rest of the world. (I'm one of them.) So there is a distinct possibility that the cashier is like me, a little bit psychic.

I try to blank my mind so that I can stand on the sidewalk and wait for my enchiladas as ethically as possible.

I thought it would be nice to surprise my wife with fancy enchiladas. The enchiladas are fancy because they cost eight dollars more here than in Redwood City, and because, _obviously_, they make you wait while they grow the corn and raise the pig. The missus can taste the difference, and I can afford upscale enchiladas for my love.

My wife likes twenty-dollar enchilada dishes and I like jogging around fancy suburbs. To be completely honest, it's the well-maintained asphalt sidewalks that reel me in. They're easier on my knees. And where the asphalt disappears and yields to unforgiving concrete? Not a problem. I can run in the street. I would never jog in the street in Redwood City. If I didn't choke on exhaust fumes, I'd be run over by a minivan and left for dead. If a Stanford person runs me over, I feel like they will probably stop. They can afford me.

I often come here, and I run around, and I dream of teaching at the university and of living in one of those big, quirky houses with skylights and a Black Lives Matter sign in the native garden out front. And then other times, I come here, and I charge down these lanes with a middle finger out on each hand, one to each row of mansions. And I'm hoping, just hoping, that some bougie fucking professor (or tech mogul) will be looking out his window as I go by. And not the gardener. I stopped doing that because of the gardeners.

Anyway, I prefer to blend in. Blending in around the univer-

> "She likes enchiladas, and I guess she likes me, but she also likes to complain about all the future versions of myself who pass her on the highway each day. 'Fucking old white men,' she snarls, and it's not like I don't understand."

sity is a hoot. I mean, I waffle about how to describe my economic situation—am I the worst version of being well-off or the best version of "broke"? Either way, I'm definitely not Stanford material. I teach ecology on an adjunct basis at a nearby community college. I have a PhD. My dad, who barely got out of high school, used me to grasp at the American dream. *You're smart*, he said. *Just keep going*, he said. *It'll pay itself back.* I grew up in the eighties. We were all "special." This is a way for me to pretend like it worked out the way my dad thought it would.

I want to tell my working-class students that it does not pay itself back. You do not keep going. But, you know, they're "special" too. So I don't say it. What I do tell them is: *be a business major and an ecology minor. Maybe you'll cancel yourself out.*

If you asked my community college students to come to Stanford Mall, and to look at the people standing on the sidewalk at this very moment—and to then identify who, out of this precise sample of people, is probably the most privileged person—I think that a lot of them would point at me. I'm the only white man. I resent that, but it's a fair guess. After all, I can afford enchiladas, and, if nothing else, ecology has taught me that you are what you eat.

But my students surprise me. They also see Gucci. They see Valley girl. They see Tesla. I'm proud of them, actually.

What does the cashier see? I focus my third eye on him, and I try to uncover his secret intentions. I try not to look like I'm straining.

But I fail. My meager mental powers cannot penetrate the cloud of his mind. No sweat. It never works that way. I've never actually succeeded at reading anyone's mind. I can only hear the echoes. I've had better success at precognition—you know, seeing the future. But that might just be my anxiety.

I've also been practicing thought implantation. I noticed that I could do this one day when I was running, in Stanford Hills, and I was almost crushed by an all-terrain stroller. I saw the thing's massive front tire coming out from behind a tall hedge a few yards ahead of me. I had a vision of trying to sidestep that tire, and of failing, and falling into the stroller. I would land on the baby, and I would poke his soft spot. The woman pushing the stroller would sue me for ruining her child. My life would be destroyed.

The vision of my doom came to me in a breath and, without really thinking, I condensed my apprehension and shot it into the woman's mind. I didn't exactly beam real words at her, but if the beam were translated into words, it would've been something like: _don't crush me._

She stopped short. She looked at me. And she quickly crossed the street.

So far, that was the only time I've been able to send telepathic transmissions. But I keep trying. Whenever I'm running around Stanford, and a Tesla or an Audi or a—what's the one with the trident-shaped emblem?—whenever one of those fucks rolls by, I tighten my brow around my third eye, I collapse my ambient negativity into a germ of anger, and I beam a thought into the driver's mind. I let him know that it's okay: _go ahead—run him over!_ I'll probably survive, and, like I said, I know they can afford me.

No one has had the guts to do it yet. Maybe it's because they're decent people. Maybe it's because I can't help but blend in. If I open my mouth, I will blend in with these people, who don't think that they have an accent. If I vote in a national election, I will blend in with these people. If I wait in line at Stanford Mall, I will blend in with everyone else who can afford fancy enchiladas. You could talk to me for a few minutes and you might even decide that I actually am Stanford material. But nobody's talking to me! *And I don't want to talk to you either.*

I know I'm a conflicted wreck, and prying my mind open isn't helping. In order to quiet my thoughts, I consciously decide that "buddy" is nothing more complicated than service with a smile. It's like one of those little tubs of mild salsa that are supposedly for white people. Most folks just throw it away, but some people will get fussy if it isn't in the bag.

While I'm waiting on the enchiladas, I look up at the moon, and I notice that there are lichens growing on the wooden beams over the sidewalk. Lichens are symbiotic combos of fungus and algae that can grow basically anywhere together. I did my dissertation on them, so I might even count as a lichen expert. I've been attracted to them ever since my undergrad days, when I learned about them in a guest lecture by—here's a coincidence—a now famous Stanford ecologist, who knew my professor at the state school. I remember the ecologist pacing in front of the projection screen, casting her shadow across images of gravestones overgrown by unruly fungal bodies. She told us that lichen colonies are effectively immortal unless they're killed. In the years since her talk, I've learned to appreciate how lichens' adaptations to rocky or broken terrain allow them to crawl up civilization's leg, to colonize everything from cemeteries to the power-washed margins of Stanford U. I hope they ride us to the moon someday.

I can't quite identify this colony from the ground, so I grab one of those wrought-iron lawn chairs that places like this use for café-style seating, and I drag it, rattling, over the concrete until it's in the middle of the sidewalk under the beams. I step up on it and I stretch my vision towards the colony. As I do so, I marvel at the privilege I'm exercising, right here in Stanford Mall! I may never go to Mars, but I thrill at the idea that I might cause a tech millionaire to take three extra steps around my nerdiness. I mean, we're all living for *his.*

In that moment, I get a psychic twinge, like a tiny electronic crackle in my brain. It's an echo of the lichen mind reaching me. No words, not even feelings, only impressions of fungal history: disparate bodies growing into one another. Colonies feeding on sunlight, and incrementally weathering the matter upon which they grow—the wood of the beams, the sidewalk concrete, the rusted-over remains of an old car. Mashing all that stuff up. Turning it into more lichen, more fungal thallus, more algae, more substrate. Hardy microscopic spores washing away in the rain, and latching onto new ground somewhere, growing, and wearing it down.

The lichen colony itself is nothing but a slight, yellow dusting, and it's hard to say because the beam is still a few feet above me, but if it's not *Chrysothrix* then it's probably *Candelariella*. The wood looks new, so maybe in a few months, these beams will have ivy on them, and the lichens will be shaded over and choked out, and the colony will die. I think, and I probably say aloud, "That's cool, that's how it goes for lichens." But I also look at them and definitely mutter, "These are my people."

A security guard comes around the corner. He's a Latino dude, half my size and maybe ten years older than me. He sees me standing on the misplaced chair and he considers me.

I am flattered. But, out of politeness, I try not to notice him. I don't want to make work for him. I clarify my situation by pulling my phone out and taking pictures of the lichen. Even though I will probably put the picture on Instagram, I concentrate on beaming the word *TikTok* into his mind.

As he walks away, it occurs to me that attempting to put my own thoughts into the security guard's mind is exactly what a white, colonial asshole would do. So, when a white man in a windbreaker approaches me, I try to implant a thought into his head too—for the sake of equity. I look down and into his face, and as he walks beneath me and by me; I seed his mind with the words: *call security*. He seems to ignore me.

Now, three teenage girls with dark hair and pink-to-light-brown skin come down the sidewalk. They are goosey, but uniform and in lockstep, walking shoulder-to-shoulder-to-shoulder in black sportswear, each eating their own fancy cupcake out of a box. One of them, the one in the middle, also has boba tea. I take a rickety attitude and I regard the girls as if they are a passing threat to my balance, which I must track until it is safe. I pick the girl in the middle to stand in for the others, and I attempt to steer her away from me with the thought: *he's gonna spill your boba!* Their single rank parts around my chair like fluid, and the girls slide by me without even looking.

Other people pass me on the chair, but security never comes back. No one nods at me or even looks at me except for the guy who sold me the enchiladas. Without me needing to ask, he says that they're on their way.

I photograph the lichens from a different angle, and then I get down and put the chair back. My enchiladas finally come up, and I wish the cashier a good night. He replies, "You too, buddy!" and I almost trip. He's definitely psychic. And I think this means we're good.

Before I go, I decide to carry out one last act of resistance, or assimilation. I go to the fancy cupcake store and I buy three, one for each girl who didn't look at me. The flavors are: s'mores, coconut crème and Black History Month. The cupcakes are expensive because it's hard to pay rent on a cupcake store anywhere near the university.

I wonder if the cupcake store in East Palo Alto also sells Black History Month cupcakes, or if their cupcakes say Black Lives Matter. But then it occurs to me what a dumb idea that is, because there is no cupcake store in East Palo Alto.

As I pay, an elderly Asian woman walks in with her three dogs, who are fancy and white-furred, and who are wearing sweaters with hoods and drawstrings. I try not to look at the dogs in the same way that I try not to look at sports cars, but then, behind her, the white man in the windbreaker comes in. I don't look at him either, but as I pass them on the way out, I hear him say to her, "Your dogs are adorable!"

I melt. I'm jealous. I wish that the seeing part of the universe had closed around me and had found *me* adorable. The guy in the windbreaker says to the lady, "I love their little sweaters."

Dejected, I load the enchiladas and the cupcakes into the car. Then I navigate out of the parking lot with great care. In the car, I am the opposite of a jogger. I cower as I pass between a Porsche SUV and one of those sinister-looking cars with the cross and the snake on the logo. I remind myself aloud that I must never surprise the drivers here. I must never honk at them. I can't afford them.

I beam soothing thoughts into their minds, and I slip away. I take everything home to my working-class, mixed-race, second-generation immigrant, white-and-API (if you like to say that) missus. We've tried out lots of words for her, and once, when one of her employers gave her a coupon, she got her DNA sequenced. We learned that on her Filipina side, her maternal haplotype is thirty thousand years of straight-up X chromosome indigeneity, and that her white family's lineage passed through knots of Russian, German and Polish identity. But who knows? She likes enchiladas, and I guess she likes me, but she also likes to complain about all the future versions of myself who pass her on the highway each day. "Fucking old white men," she snarls, and it's not like I don't understand.

We divvy up the enchiladas and she tells me about her day. She is an accomplished outdoorswoman and sometimes an adjunct professor of child development, and that is enough to convince a few of the university's worthy families to pay her part-time wages in exchange for relieving them of the burden of caring for their own preschoolers during the day. While they make fat bank or work on the cure for cancer, she takes the kids to parks and she teaches them respectful engagement with the environment. It was one of their moms who gave her the gene mapping coupons.

Today, a different mom yelled at her for letting her child get muddy again. The missus tells me that they are doing a decomposition curriculum this week, and today she taught the kids about mushrooms and lichens, and they were, naturally, on their hands and knees. The mom who complained is a tech executive, a first-generation immigrant and a first-generation rich person. She gets stressed out by dirt. Dirt isn't why she came to this country. She didn't study engineering and finance so her kid could get muddy. She is not personally interested in fungus.

I ask the professor of early childhood education who is sitting

> "...I consciously decide that 'buddy' is nothing more complicated than service with a smile. It's like one of those little tubs of mild salsa that are supposedly for white people. Most folks just throw it away, but some people will get fussy if it isn't in the bag."

across from me what she said when the mom yelled at her, and she tells me, "I just smiled."

When my wife opens the box of cupcakes, she utters a note of surprise. "This one's woke," she says. She sets the edible candy placard aside and cuts the Black History Month cupcake in half. It's meant to be Neapolitan, but it's actually chocolate cake on bottom and vanilla cake on top, with a clot of cherry goo in the middle that looks like an unresolved injury. As a model of a just society, the cupcake is disappointing.

We discuss whether or not one of us ought to write a letter to the cupcake manager about any of it. But we decide to let it go.

I pick up my half of the cupcake. I open my third eye. Does it bear the traces of its history? Is there anything in it that might betray the colonial spice trade? Anything to indicate the historical processes through which vanilla beans became the anonymous background flavor for everything sweet in the USA? Or what about the slavery that made it possible for vanilla and chocolate to become staples of northern diets? Are there echoes of triumph from civil rights activists? Is there anything in this cupcake that speaks to the sadness and anger of BLM protesters? The confusion and indignance of the police? Is there any of that in our desserts?

Nope. Obviously. I cannot mind-read a cupcake.

So, I shove my portion into my mouth. I mash up the chocolate and the vanilla and I recombine them with that sweet cherry goo.

The missus is eating her half quietly. What does she taste?

Suddenly self-conscious again, I wonder how I look as I'm cramming everything down at once. Hoping to prevent my wife from ever thinking that I'm a slob, I try to implant an alternative interpretation into her head: *he's adorable when he eats!* I beam little hearts into her eyes.

After a few seconds of that, she furrows her brow. She squints at me, and I can't tell whether she's being playful. But I can't keep up my gaze. The little hearts begin to fall into the space between us.

I'm pretty sure that she is not telepathic, per se. I feel like she's examining me. And I feel like we've got to take turns doing this. If she can read my mind, and she hasn't been telling me, well...

She doesn't stop chewing, but she actually says to me, "Oh! By the way: I never said thank you for fancy enchiladas, *buddy*!"

When Angels Speak of Love

David Harris

Sebastian dragged the old steamer trunk out of the storage closet using both arms. It was heavy and ancient, probably from the 1930s or 40s, with a rusted clasp and hinges that creaked as he lifted the lid. A musty odor penetrated his nostrils, a marker of time's passage and an earlier period in his mother's life, before he was conceived.

Beneath a pile of newspaper clippings and family photographs, he noticed a manila envelope emblazoned with the name: *Eugene*. It was the name of his deceased mother's first husband. He unwound the string clasp that held the envelope closed, pulled out a sheaf of papers and placed it on a faded oriental rug beside the trunk.

In front of him lay old tax returns, bank statements and a deed from Eugene's mother's house back in Nebraska. These were decades old and could be tossed. Then something jumped out at him: an application to adopt a child. On the second page near the bottom, he noticed two signature lines. The first, for the prospective father, was signed by Eugene in precise and formal cursive handwriting. The second, for his mother Charlotte, was blank.

Eugene's signature was dated December 15, 1987. Sebastian turned and rifled through another sheaf of papers he had found in his mother's filing cabinet a day earlier—Eugene's death certificate. He died of cardiac arrest six weeks later, in late January 1988.

Sebastian had not spent much time in this room, just above the kitchen on the second floor of his mother's house, since he packed up and left for college more than a decade earlier. He remembered it as a guest room, a den for his father and then a hobby room for his mother: quilting, needlepoint and cataloguing photos from her birding trips. It was now an ad hoc staging area as he attempted to get the house ready to sell.

Sebastian stood, walked over to the window, lifted the crusty wooden sash and stared out at the Russian River. The rolling Sonoma hills were just beyond, lush and green from the recent rains. A faint breeze blew in from the north, cooling his face, and the window's white lace curtains flapped lightly. He heard himself breathing unevenly above the sound. Though he'd been close to his mother, she rarely talked about her first marriage. He wondered if anyone still alive knew why Eugene would have wanted to adopt a child, and why his mother apparently did not.

She had passed away three months earlier, lingering for several weeks after a series of strokes, unable to move or speak, though Sebastian believed that Charlotte continued to recognize him. She had started to stabilize when a final bleed left her on life support with only her brain stem intact. As Charlotte's only child by her second marriage, and his own father having long since passed away, it was his decision to pull the plug. Though he and his mother had never discussed it, he knew it was what she would have wanted.

***

A few days later, Charlotte's younger sister, Astrid, arrived for the day. She had driven up from her home in Santa Cruz and was interested in several of Charlotte's memory quilts. Charlotte created them from pieces of clothing belonging to their parents—blue jeans and woolen plaid shirts from their father; cotton blouses, skirts and dresses from their mother. Though these quilts may have lacked something in their aesthetic beauty, Sebastian thought they more than made up for it as tangible keepsakes of his grandparents.

In Sebastian's memory, the two sisters had a close but often turbulent relationship. Astrid would turn to Charlotte when she was having one of her frequent life crises, usually involving men, jobs, friends or pets. "With Astrid, it's always something," Charlotte had sighed more than once to Sebastian, as if it were a mantra she needed to repeat to herself when her patience grew thin.

Astrid had lived with several men over the years, but never

married or had children. She often had a lot of time on her hands. After Sebastian was born, Charlotte didn't have that kind of time for her sister. Thirty years later, Sebastian could still sense from Astrid that the sting of this rejection lived on.

"I never knew about it," she told Sebastian when he showed her the adoption papers. "But it doesn't surprise me."

"I wish she had mentioned it. It hurts that she kept it hidden."

Astrid circled the room surveying Charlotte's belongings, as if she were evaluating their meaning and worth. In her early sixties, she still had a girlish quality, or perhaps, Sebastian thought, it was just an aura of immaturity. Astrid could come across like the lead character in the stage production of her own life. Any concerns beyond her own belonged to the supporting cast.

"She and Eugene were in a rough patch when he died," Astrid explained. Her voice had a world-weary quality. "Charlotte wouldn't tell me what it was, other than to say he was drinking too much and she was bored by it. I wondered if she was thinking of leaving him."

"Mom didn't talk about him much. Eugene's son, Nick, shared some things, but I met him only a few times."

"I wouldn't put much faith in what Nick told you," Astrid cautioned. "He was living proof that Eugene was lucky to have fathered only one child."

Sebastian was fifteen when Nick died in a tractor accident while helping a rancher friend near Tomales Bay. It was a Fourth of July weekend, and both had been drinking.

Sebastian remembered hearing colorful stories about Eugene from Nick. Eugene's high school students loved his humor and irreverence. Nick told him once about a taxidermied rabbit that Eugene hung from a ceiling fixture in his chemistry class. Frozen in a leaping position as if escaping from some predator, it rotated slowly throughout the day, surveying the students below, a dried rose in its mouth.

"I think your mother loved Eugene, even when he was being a pill," Astrid said. "But I can see why she might not have wanted to raise a child with him."

Charlotte once shared a story with Sebastian when he was visiting one weekend from college. Before Eugene would leave to teach his science classes in the morning, he milked their two goats, then heated some of it on the stove, poured it into a thermos and added a half an inch of vodka. He kept a pint of it in the glove compartment of his white VW bug, next to an unloaded .22 pistol.

Sebastian's own father, Marty, was less of a character. While Charlotte had never said anything to Sebastian, his sense was that her life was calmer after she married him, if not a bit duller.

"Your mom always had her reasons," Astrid said. "I didn't

always know what they were."

"Do you think my father knew about the adoption papers?"

"I doubt it."

Marty had died when Sebastian was twenty; it was a long, slow decline from lymphoma that lasted eighteen months. He was diagnosed just as Sebastian was completing his college applications.

> **"Sitting across from Astrid, he gazed at his closest living relative and realized she was all he had other than a couple of distant cousins. His father, like Sebastian, was an only child. Since Charlotte passed away, he felt alone in a new way. 'The death of the parent is also the death of the child,' a friend of Marty's told him after he died. Now he understood."**

Sebastian had wanted to attend school on the East Coast, but chose Berkeley instead. He'd taken a semester off to be with his father during those final months, and grew closer to both parents. But he wondered now what other secrets they may have taken to their graves.

Sebastian took his aunt out to lunch at his favorite place in Guerneville, the River Inn Grill. It was an old brick building, built in the late 1930s as an auto dealership, with a single, large arched window for the small showroom that was now the main dining room.

Sitting across from Astrid, he gazed at his closest living relative and realized she was all he had other than a couple of distant cousins. His father, like Sebastian, was an only child. Since Charlotte passed away, he felt alone in a new way. "The death of the parent is also the death of the child," a friend of Marty's told him after he died. Now he understood.

However, he was part of another family now—that of his wife, Olivia. They'd been married five years and his in-laws welcomed him like one of their own. They lived in northern New Jersey, and Sebastian and Olivia saw them a couple of times a year. She was from a big, raucous Irish Catholic family. All five kids had attended Catholic school. He loved the energy during the holidays, but as a product of a rural public school on the other coast, he realized early on that it was not his world.

"What do you miss most about my mom?" he asked Astrid after they had ordered their food.

"That thing that made her Charlotte. She had a spirit that I still envy. Even when things weren't easy for her, she treasured each day of her life."

"I miss that too."

"When Eugene died, and then when your father died, she just kept going. I don't know where she got it. I know *I* don't have it."

"Did you look up to her when you were younger?"

"I was jealous of her a lot of the time, so I guess so."

"She told me Grandma loved you both, maybe too much," Sebastian said.

"Maybe that's why I never married," Astrid replied. "I never moved beyond the notion of unconditional love."

Astrid picked at her large spinach salad. She'd always been a slow eater. Charlotte would comment on it whenever Astrid came over for dinner and spent the night. Sebastian finished his cheeseburger and was mopping up the drippings with his remaining french fries, then put both his hands on the table.

"Olivia and I have been talking about adopting," he announced. "We were going broke paying for fertility treatments to conceive a child on our own."

Astrid paused and looked at Sebastian, then looked out the window as if she had noticed something. "That's wonderful," Astrid said, though her tone was indifferent.

"It's what we want to do. I think it's what we *need* to do." Sebastian looked at his aunt, as if trying to gauge her reaction. "It was kind of weird to see those adoption papers, and the blank signature line above my mom's name."

"I have no doubt your mom knew what she was doing. Just think, if she had signed them, you probably wouldn't be here."

"I'd have given anything to know what was going through her mind. Eugene died six weeks after he signed them."

"She must have had her reasons," Astrid assured, repeating herself from earlier in the day. She had gone back to picking at her salad. "She always did."

41.

After Astrid left that afternoon to head back to Santa Cruz, taking several of Charlotte's quilts, Sebastian went up to the room again and continued to go through his mother's belongings. He streamed his favorite jazz station through his phone and the music kept him focused. He felt centered again. Astrid had given him a long and warm embrace when she left, tears streaming down her suntanned cheeks. It was a hug unlike any he remembered receiving from her. Perhaps they were mourning Charlotte together. They had no one else who knew their pain.

***

Sebastian said nothing to Olivia about the adoption papers he had found in the manila envelope when he got back to their home south of San Francisco that Sunday evening. He wanted to put the weekend behind him and consider in his own mind the puzzle they presented. He knew Olivia would be curious about them and what they might mean to her understanding of Charlotte. Olivia, a high school chemistry teacher with a gift for connecting to teenagers, had a strained relationship with her late mother-in-law.

"Astrid and I went out to lunch," he finally confessed as she prepared dinner, a pasta primavera recipe that she loved and Sebastian tolerated. She'd been a vegetarian for years, and food was one area of their lives that was an ongoing compromise. Sebastian's cheeseburger from lunch was still vivid in his mind. He wanted another for dinner.

"She said my mom and her first husband weren't getting along when he died. I never knew that."

She poured them a Russian River Pinot noir he brought back from Sonoma. They both took big sips while catching glances of each other, as if wary of where the conversation might lead.

"What brought that up?" Olivia asked.

"We were talking about Astrid's relationship with my mom. Eugene drank too much, which I knew. Mom told Astrid she was fed up with it when he had his heart attack."

Olivia looked into her wine glass and then toward Sebastian.

"No one likes to say this, but sometimes one spouse is better off when the other one dies." She poured the box of rigatoni into the boiling water and continued to sauté the vegetables. "I've seen that happen a few times. The surviving spouse grieves for a while and then begins to flourish."

Sebastian rolled his eyes and softly shook his head. "Good thing you never went into family counseling."

"I'd definitely be better with the kids than the parents."

"Any word from the adoption agency?"

Olivia strained the pasta and poured it into the saucepan where the tomato, broccoli, squash and carrots appeared to Sebastian a little overcooked and no longer all that suggestive of an Italian spring.

Olivia swallowed the last of her Pinot noir. "They sent me an email on Saturday. They have a few more questions. It should be only a couple more weeks before they match us with a child."

"I'm glad to hear that."

"Me too."

Sebastian poured each of them another glass of wine, finishing off the bottle. After they had eaten, he washed the dishes and Olivia streamed another episode of *Breaking Bad*. She told Sebastian she didn't like the show's violence, but was intrigued by its premise: a high school chemistry teacher is diagnosed with lung cancer. He decides he'll manufacture and sell meth with a former student to pay for treatment and provide for his family after he's gone.

"It's a case study in bad choices," she said. "Especially when you're backed up against a wall."

***

"Deadlines are the only way I get anything done," Sebastian remarked to the colleague sitting a couple of seats down from him at a long row of workstations. He had learned the previous week that her name was Leah.

"Then must have a lot of deadlines. You're always busy," she ribbed. "You've been heads down since you got here and it's three o'clock."

They were on the same team tasked with creating a software application for construction companies to price and source building materials. Sebastian liked going in on Mondays. Only a few people were in the office.

"Deadlines are great motivators," Leah added, staring at her bank of monitors. "But they don't actually do much for self-discipline in my opinion. The work still has to get done, one way or another. Am I right?"

"Yes, but a focused mind is a productive mind."

Leah countered, "Not always true—I need downtime if I'm doing anything creative."

"What do you consider 'downtime'?"

"Hanging out in the kitchen space over there and trading office gossip with colleagues."

"I'm sure I can contribute to your creative efforts then."

They bantered back and forth. He was having fun. Was she flirting with him? He noticed that her almond-shaped brown eyes were wide open and slightly mischievous as she glanced over at him. Sebastian guessed she was about his age—early thirties. She wore light green cotton pants and a yellow sweater vest over a beige blouse. Her thick, wavy brown hair rested gently on her shoulders. He liked the way she looked. She wore a simple gold wedding band on her finger.

They talked again on Friday afternoon in the kitchen area and the conversation lasted longer. Again, the office was dead. They started out on software bugs they'd solved recently—syntactic and control flow errors mostly, and a few missed commands—then on to former bosses and colleagues (admired and not), then music, then science podcasts. They discovered they were both into astronomy, and they shared photos from the James Webb Space Telescope, orbiting the sun one million miles from Earth.

"It had three hundred forty-four points of possible failure prior to launch. Did you know that?" she asked. "Places where if things didn't go as planned, it would have been a catastrophic loss."

"Think how many deadlines they must have had and how many got moved," Sebastian mused. He was looking at her wedding ring. He wondered if it was a family heirloom.

"Webb was nine billion dollars over budget and fifteen years late, but the damn thing is up there sending us images of the universe from just after the Big Bang. Can you believe it?"

"That's way before humans invented deadlines."

"We started out as space dust and we'll end up as space dust—I find that reassuring."

***

Sebastian and Olivia spent Sunday hiking on the coast near Pescadero, arriving in the late morning, just as the light coastal fog was burning off. The sun warmed the cool Pacific air and the beach below their trail lit up from faded brown to a blinding off-white.

Olivia, who was leading, stopped at a lookout and took in the panoramic view as cloud patterns painted the ocean below in shades of blue and green.

Sebastian, still thinking about what he had found in his mother's trunk, couldn't keep from wondering aloud, "What should we do if, for some reason, the adoption doesn't come through?"

"I'm not giving up," she said. "This isn't going away for me."

"Me neither."

"Why do you ask?"

He knew the answer but didn't want to say. His desire to be a parent might go away. Charlotte's unsigned adoption papers remained a mystery, not only in his mind but in his heart. How would she have lived her life if Eugene hadn't died, if she never met Marty to begin a new life?

"I just think we need to be prepared," Sebastian warned.

Neither of them looked at the other. Olivia turned and surveyed the wide expanse of water as if trying to see past the horizon. She didn't respond.

As they drove back over the coastal hills to San Mateo, he realized he was looking forward to Monday. He wanted to ask Leah what she thought about the possibility of becoming a mother, whether

"'Have you ever been unfaithful to someone you were in a relationship with?' Leah shrugged, 'In my mind, yes.' 'Do you think that's different than actually sleeping with someone?' 'I don't think a lot of marriages would last very long if they were the same thing.'"

she would ever consider adoption. Maybe that would be too forthright a question. But he wanted to know what she thought of his situation. It would be a way to get to know her better.

***

As he prepared to leave the office on Monday and head home, Leah asked him if he had time for a drink later in the week. Earlier, over lunch in the kitchen area, he had bared his soul, as much as he was prone to doing, about the adoption process. The agency was continuing to put them off, asking more questions, checking more references. He told her how Olivia's frustration and his own reticence were not mixing well. When he told Olivia he was growing bored—that was the word he used: *bored*—by the whole process, she walked into their bedroom and slammed the door. They didn't speak for the rest of the evening.

"I love her deeply, but she can be such a pain in the ass," he told Leah. He was surprised to hear these words come out of his mouth. He'd never spoken about her like that to anyone.

"It's possible to feel very lonely in a marriage," she comforted. "I know I have."

"Did it last long?"

Leah stood and grabbed a sponge from the sink, then wiped a coffee stain from the counter beside her before sitting back down at the lunch table. "Yes."

He was tempted to ask her if "yes" meant, "Yes, I'm *still* lonely." Maybe another time.

Sebastian told her about finding the adoption papers in his mother's trunk, and that ever since then his world had shifted off-center. Why had his mother never told her only son that her first marriage was so difficult?

"My father was married three times," Leah said. "Each one was less happy than the previous one—that's what he told me years later anyway. My mother was wife number two. He left her, and even though she became a single mom, I think she was relieved."

"Why couldn't he make things work with three different women?" he asked. "He must have learned *something* along the way."

"A lot of it came from his father. He was brilliant, funny, but sometimes abusive and very hard on his kids."

Sebastian probed, "But how much can somebody blame their parents' marriage for the difficulties in their own?"

"In my family, *a lot.*"

"I see the best and worst of Olivia's parents in some of her siblings. As an only child, the equation is not as clear."

***

The next weekend, he was up at Charlotte's again, and Astrid returned to help him out. She enjoyed spending time with him, he thought. That was new. With her there, however, it would be impossible to get as much work done.

One spring afternoon, when the mustard grass and poppies were blooming in tandem, Astrid queried, "Did your mom or dad say much about how they met?"

It sounded like a leading question.

"Not a lot...they met after Eugene died and fell in love very quickly. It must have been a bittersweet time for my mom."

"I think it was... For many reasons."

"They were lucky to have found each other," Sebastian said.

"Very much so," Astrid echoed.

Astrid got up from the picnic table where they were having afternoon tea, a ritual she always enjoyed, and walked around the backyard. Sebastian watched her.

"Did you know they found each other before Eugene died?" Astrid asked.

"No."

"They did. They were having an affair."

Sebastian tilted his head forward, then leaned it to the left and to the right, as if it were stiff and needed stretching. He looked up at the pale blue sky and blinked his eyes, trying to absorb what Astrid had just told him.

"Your mom made me promise before she died that I wouldn't tell you. But, after I visited you that last time, I've come around to the belief that it's something you should know."

"She was cheating on Eugene?"

Astrid started to sort through a box of family photos on the picnic table, picking out a few for an album she had mentioned wanting to put together. "*Eugene* had been unfaithful to *her* shortly after they were married. It was a rift that never healed."

Astrid said she and her sister hadn't spoken about it in years. Charlotte brought it up out of the blue a month before her stroke. It was as if she had a premonition.

"Marty was so totally charming and so different than Eugene. I could see how much happier she was and I can't begrudge her for it."

***

Sebastian returned home from work the next day to find Olivia in their bed, under the covers. She was snoring loudly as he walked in. She snorted, then turned over. He thought he heard her begin to weep. He walked over and kneeled down beside her.

"We're fucked," she whispered.

"Why?"

"The adoption fell through."

Sebastian reached over to hold her hand and she pulled it away.

Olivia rolled toward the center of the bed, away from Sebastian. After a couple of moments, she pulled off the covers and Sebastian saw she was naked. She usually slept in pajama bottoms and a t-shirt. He saw some crumbs near her shoulder, as if she had eaten something before falling asleep.

"What happened?"

Olivia rolled back over and looked Sebastian directly in the eye with a stare that drilled through his brain and right to the back of his head. Sebastian had seen this look only once before, after a fight she had with her mother.

"I was arrested for a DUI the summer I turned nineteen," she tearfully admitted. "Someone in the other car was badly hurt—a

"He recognized the recording: 'When Angels Speak of Love' by Sun Ra, who released more than a hundred jazz albums, many considered visionary by both fans and critics. Ra named himself for the Egyptian god of the sun and claimed to be an alien from Saturn on a mission to preach peace. Sebastian listened to him frequently when he was up at Charlotte's sorting through all her worldly possessions."

young boy. I've never told you about it, and I didn't say anything to the adoption agency either."

Sebastian looked at her, then down at the floor and shook his head. There were things he hadn't told her either, some much more recent. He got up and lay next to her.

"It wasn't that I had a DUI, it was that I didn't tell them about it. I didn't want to create another problem. I just wanted to put it behind me."

Sebastian leaned on an elbow and reached over to kiss her. She did not resist.

"I know it's going to be hard for you to forgive me," she said. "It's going to be hard to forgive myself."

"Let's give ourselves some time. We can try again when we feel ready."

She reached over to hold his hand. "It feels like a turning point. Like the adoption wasn't meant to happen."

He squeezed her hand back and they lay there in silence for a moment. He wasn't sure they would try again either. Even so, Sebastian consoled her. "We can find another agency. We know what they're looking for, we've got everything pulled together now."

For the first time in months, they made love. He felt more aroused than he had in a year, hungering for a connection that had seemed all but lost to him. Olivia hugged him hard as he came, but shortly afterward, she got up and went to the bathroom. He could hear her weeping but he did not get up to comfort her.

***

"Why do you think she didn't tell you?"

Sebastian and Leah were sitting outside at a patio bar near work. He decided to take her up on her offer the previous week to get a drink together.

"More than most people, she doesn't like to be embarrassed," Sebastian said. "She hates when those close to her find out something she doesn't want them to know."

"She should be embarrassed by *not* telling you. You both had so much riding on this."

He didn't want to say it out loud to Leah, but he felt that at least now he didn't need to be as truthful about himself with Olivia either.

"I found out something else recently..." Sebastian looked over one shoulder and then leaned in toward Leah. "I think I understand why my mother never signed those adoption papers."

He shared the story Nick had told him about the stuffed rabbit rotating slowly in Eugene's high school classroom. Sebastian found it both macabre and amusing, as if Eugene was trying to humor his students, as well as pique their curiosity about science, and perhaps about death.

Leah sat quietly as he grew more animated talking about Eugene, his affair shortly after marrying Charlotte, his penchant for goat's milk and vodka in the morning before heading off to teach his students.

They each ordered another drink as the sun eased down to the southwest, eventually dipping beneath the hills between San Mateo and the coast. He knew Olivia was at a school board meeting and that those often ran well past nine-thirty.

"Have you ever been unfaithful to someone you were in a relationship with?"

Leah shrugged, "In my mind, yes."

"Do you think that's different than actually sleeping with someone?"

"I don't think a lot of marriages would last very long if they were the same thing."

"My parents had more complicated lives than I ever imagined," Sebastian said. "Do we repeat the same patterns even if we never knew the patterns existed in the first place?"

He remembered his dad's struggle with lymphoma. His mother would sit by his father's bed for hours as he slept. She knitted and read, but mostly she just sat with him.

"I like to think we have a choice in how we act, but I'm not sure," Leah mused. "Sometimes there's an inevitability to things."

She picked up her mojito and swirled the ice and mint around, then sipped what remained.

"Do you think you'll stay with your husband?"

She removed her sunglasses from the table and put them in her handbag. "It depends on the day of the week. When I'm sitting here with you, it makes it harder. But maybe I'm just acting out."

The waiter walked over and asked if they wanted another drink.

"We'll take the check," Leah asserted.

Neither of them spoke as they walked out to the parking lot. Sebastian was thinking of the last woman he had slept with before Olivia. He had dated her in college, then fell out of touch with her; they had a fling several years later during a brief breakup with Olivia. After two mojitos, he was in the mood.

Inhibitions lost, he turned toward Leah and put his arms around her. "Let's a get a motel room for a couple of hours—what do you think?"

She rested her head on his shoulder and they swayed back and forth. "I like that idea, but I'm going to say no."

"At this very moment, that doesn't make sense."

"It doesn't have to."

He wondered how much he still loved Olivia. With Charlotte gone, he felt untethered to the world. Now he wanted to float free of it.

***

When he got home, he noticed that the air conditioning and the fans had been turned off, and that a few of the windows were open. The nearby freeway created a low humming noise throughout the apartment that he wasn't used to. He entered the kitchen, opened the refrigerator, then looked at the stove. There was no sign that Olivia had eaten anything. He thought she should be home from the meeting by now and walked into their bedroom to see if she was in there reading, or perhaps had fallen asleep. Instead, he caught sight of a handwritten note on his nightstand that read:

I need to go away and get some clarity on us. Taking two weeks and will be at my sister's on the Jersey shore. This will be good for you too. I still love you but there's static coming from somewhere—for both of us. You feel that too, right? I think it's why I screwed up on the DUI stuff. I'll call you in a few days. Love, O.

He stared at the note, reread it a couple of times, then turned toward the old Sony AM-FM radio that he and Olivia bought at Goodwill when they first moved in together. She had tuned it to the same jazz station he streamed on his phone at his mother's. He recognized the recording: "When Angels Speak of Love" by Sun Ra, who released more than a hundred jazz albums, many considered visionary by both fans and critics. Ra named himself for the Egyptian god of the sun and claimed to be an alien from Saturn on a mission to preach peace. Sebastian listened to him frequently when he was up at Charlotte's sorting through all her worldly possessions. This recording was among his favorites. It calmed his mind and his body. He read an article recently that Ra said his music, at its core, was about happiness. Charlotte would have understood. Maybe someday Olivia would too.

Bromius at the Beach

Steve Fromm

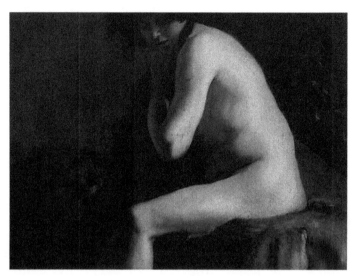

"**I**'ll give you the tour."

Claire greeted Cass at the front door, cheerily introduced herself and then hit her with a litany of questions: *Trouble finding the place? First time in Dewey Beach? How long are you staying?*

No. Yes. One week.

Cass was still standing at the door and already wanted to avoid Claire. She wasn't much on tours, and even less on people eager to give them. It wasn't even Claire's house. It was a beach rental. That made it worse.

"Living room," Claire said as they entered a large, airy space filled with light, a small bar and pastel furniture. Cass' eyes went to a sliding glass door that led to a deck and then still farther out to a patch of switchgrass and then the wide, blue ocean.

"Very nice," Cass complimented.

"French oak," Claire replied.

"Excuse me?"

"The floor," Claire said, looking down. "French oak. Beautiful shade that really adds to the sense of light."

"French oak," Cass repeated. "Very nice."

They continued to the kitchen. Claire opened the refrigerator. "We have a shelf arrangement," she explained.

"I'm sorry?"

"The shelves. I have the middle. You can have the bottom. *She* has the top."

Cass didn't ask about the *she*. Claire would get to her soon enough. They turned out of the kitchen into a narrow hallway.

"Bedrooms," Claire pointed. "I'm here. Yours is next. Then hers. In back."

Cass peered in at her bedroom. It looked the same as what was shown on the internet: king-sized bed, bureau, lounge chair, flatscreen TV, wide window with a beach view. Claire then showed her the bathroom, across from the bedroom. There was a similar arrangement with the medicine cabinet shelves. Claire had her things on the top two shelves.

"Eleanor," Claire seemed to say apropos of nothing as they walked back to the living room.

"Who?"

"Number three. Her name is Eleanor. Ran into her once since I got here. That was four days ago."

"Once?"

"She's got her own."

Cass looked at her.

"Bathroom. Back there."

"I see."

"She went out a while ago. I don't know where."

"Mm," Cass said, walking back to the front door to retrieve her luggage. Claire was right behind her. She grabbed one of the bags. They started toward Cass' room.

"It's not that she's unfriendly," Claire continued. "Nothing like that. It's just she doesn't—"

She stopped there, as if Cass understood. She did. Completely. They put the bags down in Cass' room. Claire stood there as if waiting for a tip.

Instead, Cass nudged her to leave. "Well... Thank you."

"Sure."

Cass walked over to the bedroom door and waited.

Before exiting, Claire turned around. "Sure. Sure thing," she added again. Then: "I'll be heading out for a drink soon."

Cass didn't answer.

"Okay," Claire said. "See you soon."

Cass closed the door and unpacked. It didn't take long. She'd always been a light traveler. She put her bathroom things at the foot of the bed, then walked over to the window and watched the waves roll in, low and gentle. It was late afternoon. People were rolling up their umbrellas, folding their chairs and trudging their way through the sand.

Cass heard footsteps in the hallway. The front door opened and shut. She gathered her toiletries, went to the bathroom and placed the items on the bottom two shelves. After she was done, she turned down the hall and walked to the back bedroom. The door was closed. Cass placed her hand on the doorknob, but didn't turn it. She stood there for a few moments before returning to her own bedroom.

***

"So. What the hell is an error theorist?"

Cass had risen early that morning, gone for a long run on the beach, then installed herself on the deck, sipping coffee and watching the sun rise. She was hoping for ninety minutes of peace. She got an hour. Claire emerged from the house, coffee in hand, plunked herself down and proceeded to regale her with last night's adventures.

"Good-looking guy," Claire remarked. "Nice smile. And his nails."

"Nails?"

"First thing I look at when I check out a guy," she said. "If they're long and dirty, forget it. I mean, if he's that way with his nails, what's the rest like?"

"I see."

"So we talk. I tell him about my real estate business, the hot markets, fixed-rate mortgages, that kind of thing. And he tells me he's an *error theorist*. I didn't ask. I'll Google it later. I shouldn't be embarrassed. Who knows—"

"It's a theory concerning the validity of moral judgment," Cass interjected. "It deals with the possibility that morality is a delusion that helps us get through the day."

Claire looked at her incredulously.

"I read a lot," Cass shrugged.

Claire took a quick sip of coffee. "Reading. Wish I had time. What with the business and all, I'm lucky to get a week down here."

Claire kept talking. Cass nodded now and again, but she wasn't listening. She was staring out at the surfers, twisting and turning on middling waves, then out still further to the hazy reaches of the horizon.

Claire asked a question that Cass was forced to tune back in for.

"Meet her yet?"

"Eleanor? No."

"She came in last night." Claire paused. "Real late."

Cass didn't answer. Claire hung on for a while longer, sipping her coffee and trotting out different strands of conversation. None of them took. She finished her coffee and stood. "Heading to the beach?"

"Not now. Maybe later."

"I like it in the morning. Too hot past noon."

Cass gave her a cursory *mm-hm*, then reached for a book she'd brought out to the deck. Mercifully, Claire didn't ask about the title and disappeared into the house. Once she was gone, Cass put down the book, picked up her coffee and stared out at nothing. After Claire departed for the beach, Cass went in and took a shower. On the way back to her room, she heard a voice coming from Eleanor's room. The tone was harsh, but she couldn't make out the words. She took a few steps closer and listened.

"Arthur? *Arthur*. What did I tell you? Good. Now repeat it. Repeat it again. Good. Very good, Arthur. I'll expect it tomorrow. *Then* I'll deal with you."

The conversation ended. Cass went back to her room. She dressed in shorts, a t-shirt and sandals, then headed out to a small grocery store at the end of the street. She bought a few essentials and two bottles of white Bordeaux from a liquor store next to the grocery. When she returned to the beach house, there was still no sign of Claire. She put the groceries away, poured herself another cup of coffee and went out to the deck.

The beach was dotted with clusters of umbrellas and blankets, the gulls swooping in for pieces of bread and discarded fruit as children kicked soccer balls and flicked Frisbees. Cass' vision settled on a woman striding toward the water. She had mid-length, dark brown hair with caramel highlights and wore a black one-piece with high-cut hips. A man under a nearby umbrella looked up from his book as she walked by. He kept looking.

Cass watched as the woman waded into the surf and then dove deftly into the base of an incoming wave. She resurfaced on the other side, whipped her hair back and dove under the next one. When she hit calmer water, she broke into a smooth crawl until she was still further out. A lifeguard blew her whistle and made a motion. The woman swam out several more yards. The lifeguard blew her whistle again. The swimmer turned and headed back in. Cass watched a while longer but didn't wait for her to reach the beach. She knew it was Eleanor.

***

Claire went out that evening with the error theorist, dressed in a little black dress and smelling of Paco Rabanne.

"Wish me luck."

Cass nodded. "Very best."

After Claire left, Cass took a long shower to wash off the oil and sweat from a day laying out on the beach, grabbed another glass of Bordeaux and her book, then walked to a nearby Korean restaurant specializing in *tteok-bokki*. It was cool and dark inside, too dark to read, but that didn't bother her. The book was mainly a prop when she went out alone. She lingered there for a while, consuming most of the bottle.

When she returned to the house, she found only the lingering scent of Claire's perfume. She uncorked the wine, poured the remainder into a glass and walked out to the deck. Cass took a sip, placed the glass on the railing and looked at the ocean, a sliver of moon casting a silvery tint over the calm water.

"Hey," a voice greeted.

Cass turned toward the table. A lighter flared, momentarily, revealing a flash of tanned, angular cheekbones.

"Hi," Cass said.

"You must be the third inmate."

"I am."

"Arrive yesterday?"

"Yes. In the afternoon."

"Get the tour?"

Cass smiled. "Yeah."

The red tip of the cigarette made a little arcing motion. "Why don't you sit down?"

"Sure," Cass agreed, picking up her glass and making her way to the lounge chair next to Eleanor. Once she sat down, she introduced herself. "I'm Cassidy."

"Eleanor."

Cass got a closer look at the high cheekbones, rounded nose and large eyes that colored brown when Eleanor took a drag and the ember flared. It wasn't a cigarette.

Eleanor offered the joint to Cass. "Northern Lights. Undertones of lemon. Not sure if it'll clash with your wine."

"I'll take the chance," Cass said, enjoying a few hits before giving it back to Eleanor.

"Where's Claire?"

"Out. On a date."

"Splendid. When it comes to Claire, I'm a minimalist."

Cass laughed and reached for the joint again. They picked at Claire for a bit longer until the conversation hit its own rhythm, moving on to how long they were staying, the best restaurants in the vicinity and the difficulty of finding rentals in that area, leading them both to a house-sharing option.

"What do you do, Cassidy?"

"Cass. Attorney. Intellectual property."

"You like it?"

"No. Not really. But business is..." She stopped there, looking for the right word. "Burgeoning."

They talked more. Cass wanted to turn the conversation to Eleanor's own burgeoning business, but couldn't think of a tactful way. After several minutes, Eleanor looked at her phone and got up from her seat.

"Gotta go. Have to make some calls. Maybe we can go to the beach tomorrow."

"Sounds good." Cass thought a moment. "What about—"

"'And he tells me he's an *error theorist*. I didn't ask. I'll Google it later. I shouldn't be embarrassed. Who knows—' 'It's a theory concerning the validity of moral judgment,' Cass interjected. 'It deals with the possibility that morality is a delusion that helps us get through the day.'"

"Claire?"

"Yeah."

"We'll figure something out," Eleanor said with a smile.

Cass finished her wine, then went to the kitchen. She felt high and a bit outside herself as she washed the glass. On the way to her bedroom, she picked up on Eleanor's voice. She took a few steps toward the back bedroom door.

"Desmond. You know that excuse doesn't work with me. You *know* this. So what am I supposed to do with you? Not enough. Not *nearly* enough."

Cass went into her bedroom and closed the door. She stripped and sprawled onto her bed in the dark. The bed began spinning counter-clockwise. She got up and went to the window. There was no moon. The ocean was black. Cass laid down again. The bed didn't spin. She listened for Eleanor's voice but couldn't hear it. Cass closed her eyes. She tried to sleep.

***

Cass went out to the deck early next morning, grateful that the wine and weed hadn't left any traces. Claire came out thirty minutes later. She looked less fortunate. Her complexion was off and her eyes bloodshot. Coffee slopped out of her mug when she put it on the table.

"How'd it go?" Cass asked.

Claire waited a moment. "Not well."

"I see."

Though she didn't ask for more details, it didn't stop Claire from giving them. She described her date for the next ten minutes. *All* of it.

"I mean, he tells me this. He *blurts* it right out."

"Maybe he was drunk."

"We were only two glasses into a bottle of Rombauer," Claire countered, taking a sip of coffee. "I mean, are men *really* into that? Or maybe he's never done it, but *thinks* he'd be into it?"

"I don't—"

"How could he just come out and say that on our first real date? He looks so normal."

"Are you going to see him again?"

Claire shot her a look. They went silent. The beach was still empty, except for the occasional runner. They drank their coffee and listened to the waves and gulls. Claire murmured something unintelligible to Cass.

"What?"

"I'm leaving," Claire repeated. "Today."

She looked at Cass as if waiting to be argued out of it. Cass didn't say anything, but got up to get more coffee. When she returned to the deck, Claire was gone.

***

Cass and Eleanor went out to the beach later that morning.

"Claire's gone?" Eleanor asked.

"Yes."

"What happened?"

"An error theorist."

"Huh?"

"She hooked up with an error theorist. Apparently, it was an error."

Eleanor laughed, but didn't ask any further questions.

Cass led them tso the spot on the beach where she'd gone the day before. They anchored Eleanor's umbrella, spread out the blanket, methodically covered themselves with sunscreen and settled in. The lifeguards were already on duty, and several umbrellas had sprouted up around them. A welter of screaming kids were sliding and swerving into the water with their boogie boards.

Eleanor stood up. "Going in?"

"Not yet."

"Okay. See you in a bit."

Eleanor waded in and started swimming. Cass raised herself on her elbows and watched. Eleanor didn't go as far out as she had the other day, lulling on her back in the calm water. Cass sensed someone watching her and looked to her left. Two men were sitting on towels, one with aviators, the other with a backwards baseball cap. Aviators was looking right at her. He smiled. Cass looked back at the ocean. Eleanor was heading ashore, gaining her feet in the surf. She was back at their umbrella in another minute, smoothing her hair back and wringing it.

"How's the water?"

"Brisk."

Eleanor stared at Cass' hair. "I've been thinking about that. Cutting it short."

"Always liked it this way. Easier to handle."

"Such a light blonde," Eleanor said, laying on her stomach.

"Yeah. Gets lighter in the summer."

Aviators was still taking them in. Eleanor noticed. He shot her a smile.

"Ugh."

"What?"

"The smile. We all know what that means."

"How long?"

"A minute. Maybe two," Eleanor predicted.

Two minutes later, Aviators got up and walked over to them.

"Morning, ladies."

"Morning," Cass returned.

Eleanor didn't answer. Her eyes were closed.

"Up for some paddle ball?"

"Not right now, thank you," Cass said.

Aviators pressed, "Maybe in a bit? You know. Gets the blood moving."

Eleanor's eyes remained closed. "Our blood is moving just fine."

"C'mon," he urged, looking at Cass. "We can do a three-way." He used the word "three-way" with a deliberately suggestive tone.

Eleanor raised her head. "You're not much on respecting privacy, are you?"

"I'm kind of an agnostic on the issue," he replied. He thought it was clever. Cass wondered how many times he'd used it.

"Colloquial or classic?" Eleanor demanded.

"Huh?"

"Your use of agnostic. Do you mean in a colloquial or classic sense?"

Aviators' expression slipped for a split second. Cass saw it. Aviators didn't realize it, but he was already a ghost.

"Tell you what. Go back to your little towel over there and look up agnostic. You can learn all you need to know about the word before you attempt to use it again."

"'I go for the multiples.' 'Multiples?' 'Screen names with a sense they're leading multiple lives.' 'Why?' 'Safer. Or it *feels* safer, like they've got something to lose. They all do. And most *are* leading multiple lives.'"

Aviators stood there for a few moments, gawking at Eleanor, who'd lowered her head and closed her eyes again. Cass kept her lips straight and stared out at the ocean. A word came to her: *defenestration*. Aviators went back to his blanket. He didn't look at them again.

Eleanor grunted. "Amusement park."

"What?"

"Guys like him. They think the world's an amusement park, and *we're* the rides."

Cass looked down at Eleanor. Her eyes were closed again.

They stayed on the beach until mid-afternoon, intermittently swimming and laying out in the sun. After eating some fruit and yogurt, they fell asleep. When Cass awoke, Eleanor was already up, rolling the towels.

"What time?"

"About three," Eleanor said. "I'm late. Have to make some client calls."

Cass got to her feet, stretched and helped pack. She looked around. Aviators and his pal were long gone.

"You have plans for dinner?" Eleanor asked as they walked back to the house.

"Not really."

"I know a good seafood place. Hake bobotie, tuna ceviche. That kind of thing."

"Sounds interesting."

"Seven good?"

"Seven. Sure."

Eleanor's phone chimed as they were climbing the stairs to the deck. She swiped into the call.

"Robert? Call back in five minutes. *Precisely* five minutes."

She ended the call. Cass acted as if she hadn't heard.

***

"It's very polite," Eleanor said.

"Hm?"

"You not asking. About what I do."

They were seated at a back table in the seafood restaurant, splitting a crab crostini appetizer and a bottle of Pahlmeyer after putting in their orders.

"It's a big beach house, but not that big," Eleanor continued. "I know you've heard my conversations."

"Yes," Cass conceded as she picked up a piece of crostini. "I've heard."

"We don't have to talk about it if you don't want to."

"No. I *am* curious."

The waiter appeared and refilled their glasses, then stepped away.

"How do you meet them?" Cass asked.

"Online. Platforms that focus on mutual interests."

"How do you determine—"

"How much?"

"Yes."

"I let them know *exactly* what I expect. They can take it or leave it."

"And they always take it?"

"Almost. It doesn't matter if they don't. There are so many of them."

"What happens after you agree on an arrangement?"

"We finalize the finances, the information and all that, and then we start."

"That's it?"

"That's it."

"I don't know," Cass said. "I've heard bits of what you do. It sounds—"

"Intense?"

"More like exhausting."

The waiter reappeared with their food, asked if they needed anything, then left again.

"It's not. *They* do most of the work. It's all about what they want me to be. They *create* me."

"You mean like projecting?"

"Yes. The challenge is not doing too much, to stay within the bounds of what they think I am."

"And for that they—" Cass stopped.

"Yes."

"I wonder how it starts in them. That need."

"All I know is it's there. And it won't leave them alone."

They ate, ordered another bottle of wine and split a raspberry sorbet for dessert. Eleanor kept talking. Cass listened to the list of clients. Desmond, Robert, Arthur and more. Many more. Preston. Richard. Gerald. Gideon. Sterling. Eleanor didn't go into how much they paid or precisely what they paid for, and Cass knew not to ask.

They finished the second bottle of wine. Eleanor picked up the check. Cass left the tip. They wandered around town for a while, stopping to browse at a vintage record store and then an antique shop before heading back to the beach house.

Eleanor laid out a clear plan: "I'll get the weed, you get the wine. Meet you on the deck."

Cass opened the fridge and found a bottle of Pinot on Claire's abandoned shelf. She opened it and put the bottle and two glasses on a tray rummaged from a cabinet above the sink, then carried them to the deck. Eleanor was already there, rolling a joint.

"Northern Lights?"

"No. Tangie. Kind of like tangerine. You'll like it."

Cass poured the wine. Eleanor lit up, took a hit and passed it over. They sat in silence for a while, enjoying a cool breeze coasting in from the dark water. Eleanor's phone was on the table, next to her wine. It chimed. She ignored it.

"How do you choose?"

"Clients? They post profiles. You look for certain things. What they do. How badly they want it. That kind of thing."

"What if they're all about the same?"

"It can get arbitrary. I may choose from the screen names. I go for the multiples."

"Multiples?"

"Screen names with a sense that they're leading multiple lives."

"Why?"

"Safer. Or it *feels* safer, like they've got something to lose. They all do. And most *are* leading multiple lives."

"What are some of the screen names?"

"Lots of Jekyll and Hyde variations. Then there are versions on polycephaly. Multiple heads."

Eleanor's phone chimed again. She dimmed the screen, rolled another joint and lit up. They talked some more, feeling light and loose.

Eleanor started reciting some of the screen names. "Myriad. Aberration. Doublet."

They laughed.

"Vizard. Dyad. Multifarious," Eleanor rattled off, picking up her glass and holding it like an offering to the gods. "Dichotomous. Anomaly. Multitudinal."

"Is that last one a word?"

"Yes."

"Awful."

"Some go in for the mythology. The twins. Apollo and Artemis. Hypnos and Thanatos. Phobos and Deimos."

"I like those," Cass said.

"Yes. A bit more style."

"Style... A bit more style."

Cass reached for the joint. Eleanor handed it over. Cass took a deep hit and passed it back. She waited a few moments, then let out a long stream of grayish smoke.

"How about this for style," Cass said. "Bromius."

Their eyes met over the table.

"Bromius," Cass repeated. "Ever come across that one?"

"Bromius," Eleanor echoed.

"Otherwise known as Dionysus. Or Evius. Or Bacchus. The masked god. How's *that* for a multiple?"

Eleanor held the burning joint, but her hand didn't move. She was staring at Cass.

"Need something a bit more specific? Bromius814. That ring a bell?"

Eleanor blinked.

"Know what the 814 stands for? I do. August 14. That's our anniversary."

Eleanor's phone chimed.

"You going to get that? Maybe it's Artemis or Phobos or Deimos."

Eleanor didn't reach for the phone.

"It's not Bromius. He's somewhere else. Want to know where?"

Eleanor didn't answer. She seemed to be looking at a spot just above Cass's head.

"He's alone, in a grimy studio apartment. It's his new home. He doesn't see anyone, except a therapist. A *real* therapist."

Cass reached over, snatched the joint from Eleanor's fingers and inhaled. "Tangy. Like tangerines."

Duncan. Duncan with his secrets. He kept them well. Savings gone. IRA gone. Investment account gone. Proceeds from a covert second mortgage, gone. Duncan. Gone. All that was left were emails and texts, little pieces leading to an overpriced beach rental and a deck reeking of weed.

Cass took another hit and put the joint on the table. Eleanor stayed silent. She was looking at the joint. Cass took the bottle of wine and emptied what was left into her glass, then held it. "Here's to amusement parks. Amusement parks and rides."

She drained the glass and tossed it over the deck railing. It didn't make a sound. Cass got up. She wasn't looking at Eleanor. She went down the deck stairs to the beach, then to where the water rolled in. She started walking. It was dark and breezy and the cold water felt good around her ankles and calves.

Cass didn't know how long she walked. By the time she returned, the horizon was showing the first traces of a chalky dawn. She walked up the deck stairs and into the house. As she went to her bedroom, she saw that Eleanor's door was open. She peered in. The room was empty, with an unmade bed and the closet door ajar. Cass went to her room, closed the door and locked it. She fell into bed without undressing and closed her eyes. She knew sleep would come. She knew that for the first time in a long while, it would come fast.

This Was War

E.P. Lande

"It's *soooo* good to see ya. It seems like we haven't danced in, I don't know, forever."

It was Tuesday, and Katie was back. She had taken a break from our Argentine tango lessons, during which time she spent a week at Kripalu, a yoga retreat in the Berkshires. Before Katie left, she told me she needed a break from relationships. But now that she had returned, I could take a victory lap with her in my arms, what with having successfully undermined her affair with Barry.

She looked radiant, really quite seductive. She had a glint in her eye, and she moved with cat-like grace. Our dancing seemed, well, better tuned. Katie followed my lead without any effort, like we had been dancing forever. She glided over the floor, embellishing her moves with precise *boléos*, and when I led a gancho, her hook was sharp and graceful. Perhaps the retreat to Kripalu was just what she needed.

"I had such a good time...and guess what?"

I pulled back from our embrace. I looked closely and saw something different in her eyes, a far-off expression, almost a glazed-over stare, but I knew she wasn't on anything.

Then it hit me. "No Katie. *No*. It can't be. It's not..."

"Yes...*yes!*"

"Katie, you can't be serious. Don't you remember what you told me only last week? That you were through with involvements, that you needed a break from entanglements, that dating would be a relief from messy intimate relationships? And that was barely a week ago. Katie, don't you remember?"

"Oh, but sweetie, that was before I met *Josh*."

"But what about the break you mentioned? What about that?"

Was Katie's private life beginning to interfere with our dancing?

"I took my break. It's been over a week since I ended things with Barry."

I definitely needed a course in understanding women. How could I argue with such logic? What would be the point? I held Katie in my arms, and we began dancing. She was sensual; her body spoke of emotions I had yet to taste, of experiences I might dream, whose existence for me lay somewhere, to be had—perhaps. I couldn't explain, but I wasn't defeated. I had gone up against Barry and won that battle. Now it seemed I'd be confronted with a second. This was war.

"I invited Josh for the holidays," Katie noted casually as she gancho'd between my legs. "You'll like Josh, I know you will."

...And I know I won't.

I tried not to be distracted by Katie's announcement and the approaching battle. Christmas was only three weeks away. During Christmas, I would implement a plan to eliminate Josh.

***

I didn't meet Josh until he showed up with Katie at the restaurant. He was young, but unexpectedly good-looking. He was *too* good-looking. My sense of aesthetics would be working against me. I had to concentrate my scheming on something else—like character. I wasn't sure how this would fit into my plan, but possibly his personality flaws would offset his looks. I began thinking diabolic thoughts—a specialty of mine. Maybe I was jealous—until I remembered: this was war.

Running through my mind at that moment was W. Somerset Maugham's story, "The Point of Honor," about a Spanish aristocrat who, despite his liking the man he believed rivaled him for the affections of his wife, felt he had to kill him in a duel to protect his—and his wife's—honor. I had only just met Josh. He seemed like a decent chap, giving me a pang of guilt for what I felt I had to do.

Katie looked very charming in an alpaca woolen skirt with an Inca-inspired motif, an ice blue jersey top and stilettos. Very light makeup highlighted her youthful face. After I seated her and Josh, I sent Chad, their waiter for the night, to their table. Katie was a half-a-glass-of-wine-an-evening drinker. In the past, I had suggested that she shouldn't drink even half a glass when we were dancing, as it threw her off her balance.

I knew I could count on Chad to be loud and obvious...and he was. When he asked Josh for his ID, Josh's complexion turned beet red. Rattled, he had difficulty locating his driver's license, fumbling in the process. His face contorted as he panicked. In the meantime, Chad flirted ostentatiously (but innocently) with Katie, who he had known since her first appearance in the restaurant months before.

Drink orders taken, I watched as Josh, in a high state of animation, not to say agitation, became very vocal—almost babbling —while conversing with Katie, who remained calm, as though this was her date's normal behavior...and perhaps it was. Had I gone too far? I didn't know Josh, and now I was beginning to feel remorse. What had I done?

After giving him sufficient time to fully absorb the blow that had been delivered—and myself time to recapture my host's composure— I walked over to where they were sitting. Now was the time for me to be welcoming; I had made my thrust, albeit via Chad.

"Hi kids, everything okay?"

"Hi! Everything is fine. Josh got a little flustered when Chad asked to see his ID. I guess in New York, he's not used to having to show it. Fortunately, he had one, otherwise it might have been a lemonade night."

At this point, the shade of crimson in Josh's complexion darkened and Katie gave me one of her mischievous smiles that told me she was having a wonderful time.

I sat with them for a few minutes. I wanted to become acquainted with Josh...maybe I could discover what made him interesting to Katie. He taught history and English at a New York high school, two subjects that I not only enjoyed during my pre-university years, but still did. It appeared that Josh and I had quite a lot in common; I was starting to think I might be willing to convince him to take up tango...quickly followed by another thought warning me that I should wait before offering. Perhaps later, when we got to know one another better—if later ever arrived.

"Josh, since you teach grammar, I've been told I use ellipses far too often..."

"Funny that you ask about ellipses, Aaron. My students hardly ever use them...and when they do, they invariably get them wrong."

If I'm not mistaken, Josh just made the mistake I've so often been accused of.

"If you're around tomorrow, perhaps Katie can bring you over."

"Tomorrow should work for us."

"Great. Well, I've got to get back to work. Have fun tonight."

Josh might be able to punctuate his lines correctly, but I was just beginning to master the art of creating footnotes.

***

Everyone was dancing. Not necessarily the tango, but they were enjoying themselves. The staff moved the tables and chairs to the sides to make more room. I offered Josh the opportunity to dance with Katie, but he refused, saying he was only interested in swing, East Coast swing. So I danced with Katie, who had drunk her half-glass of wine and was somewhat unsteady.

"You know, my love, you shouldn't drink and dance. I've warned you before."

"Oh, sweetie, I'm having such a lovely time, a little wine won't hurt." She rested her head on my chest without my encouragement.

"It won't hurt, but you forget how to follow." I held her tight, in a close embrace, almost lifting her off her feet so that following was less of an issue. "I think Josh is kinda nice."

"I'm glad you think so, sweetie, 'cause I trust your opinion."

We continued dancing...more like walking actually, as there wasn't room on the dance floor to do more than that. My thoughts floated to how it would be, just Katie and me. No Barrys or Joshes to eliminate. No scheming. Just a normal life caring for each other, a time when it's Tuesday every day of the week—always.

"Josh is younger than me, you know," she murmured.

"Yes, you told me, but the two of you look, well, nice together." It was New Year's, so I could afford to be out of character—for one night.

***

The Tuesday after New Year's, I held Katie in my arms, dancing in my restaurant.

"Katie, you feel out of breath."

"Why do you say that?"

"'Cause I can feel it, in your body."

"You mean, because my chest is heaving?" As Katie said this, I observed one of those very cat-like, almost carnal smiles begin to spread across her face, from cherished ear to cherished ear.

"Yes," I answered...and immediately knew I shouldn't have.

"He *is* cute, don't you think?"

Katie started to move slowly, to sway really, pendulating from one leg to the other, her hips rhythmically oscillating. And as she did, her body changed, blending into mine.

"I agree. Actually, Josh is good-looking." I meant what I said... because it was true, because it was obvious. If I wanted to eliminate Josh—and I did—I would have to concentrate my efforts on his Achilles' heel, not downplay his better attributes.

"Katie, are you thinking rationally? Do you really want another child on your hands?"

Her body continued swaying in time to the rhythm—slow and sensual. "But, sweetie... Okay, you're right. Josh is rather handsome—but I also think he's cute."

End of discussion.

We danced and made plans for Josh's eventual (and inevitable) return. Fortunately, school for him began immediately after the New

"I began thinking diabolic thoughts—a specialty of mine. Maybe I was jealous—until I remembered: *this was war.*"

Year; he would be busy until Martin Luther King Jr. Day. But that was barely three weeks off. I would probably have her mooning over this half grown-up for the next few weeks. Recalling Sun Tzu, the supreme art of war is to subdue the enemy without fighting. I would call upon my shored-up patience—a necessity in battle.

"What do you two have in common, if I may ask?" *Did I sound sardonic?*

"Well, we didn't have that much time to discuss topics of mutual interest."

Here I felt a tinge, just a tinge, of the need to fight back, to defend her turf—that is, if I could call Josh "turf."

She continued, "Don't forget, we did meet at Kripalu, so we have that in common."

Yeah, I forgot—stretching. "Does Josh meditate?" For that matter, did Katie? But I judiciously avoided asking.

"No, I don't think so. He seems too mellow as it is. Meditation would probably be soporific for Josh, you know—I mean, he doesn't seem to have any issues."

Maybe that's his problem: no issues. If he had any, he might be more interesting.

"No issues, eh? That's, well...he's lucky. Maybe I should take a few lessons from him myself—to get rid of a few of my own." Now I was being a little too cynical—even for me.

"Oh, sweetie, I *love* your issues. You don't have to get rid of any."

Short of Katie telling me I was just about perfect, how could I dispute what she had just said? "Yeah, issues make you interesting, I guess. It's like having character...or morality." Now I was moving into deep waters; I had better be careful.

"I don't know about morality—but character, yes, I agree. Maybe that's where Josh is a little deficient. He's somewhat...blah. You know, monochromatic."

Now there, Katie had a point. She just gave me the key to Josh's Achilles' heel. Katie loved my issues—which I'd have to think about so that I could display them more often when I was with her—and she didn't find that Josh had many, if *any* at all. Did Katie prefer a person with issues—regardless of what they were—or someone devoid of them? *That* I would have to explore...and then exploit.

"Josh isn't all that bad," I assured. "And he can swing dance, East Coast-style." I laid it on thick, adding, "Josh made a good first impression on me. I look forward to spending more time with him, like when we discussed grammatical forms. Assuming he returns, of course." There, that should earn me some points—for fairness.

"Sweetie, you can be *soooo* unselfish. It's one of the traits I just *adore* about you. You know that, don't you? That you can be generous, almost too generous. And not just when you want to be."

How could I argue, or even think of disputing Katie's reasoning? It's also what so endeared her to me. She made me feel like the Sir Galahad I wished to be, but I couldn't tell her.

"You know, I think Josh is a teeny bit jealous of you," Katie admitted in a muffled tone as her head rested on my chest, the *bandoneón* wailing of unrequited love, lost, never to return. In our close embrace, Katie felt soft, vulnerable, as we moved gently over the notes, dancing as though the dance floor were crowded, the music urging us to linger, not to rush. I led her to step over my right foot—a simple step, to break the flow.

"Jealous? Of me? What for?" I could think of a whole bunch of reasons, but my thoughts were somewhere else. After almost a year, I couldn't tell if Katie was truly aware of my feelings for her. Or if I even knew what they were myself. I had to admit, I still lacked the courage to acknowledge them, even in the privacy of my own bedroom.

"Well, for one, I talk about you, *a lot*...like all the time."

Perhaps I could guide the course of the discussion closer to my unexpressed goal—but, what *was* my goal? For the moment, I meant to derail Josh while keeping *my* train on track. A violin picked up the theme of thirsting for love, perhaps fleeting.

I kept the conversation topic going. "But, that's only natural. I mean, I'm here because Barry wanted you to learn tango, and I'm *still* here—even though he isn't—because you like to dance—and I'm the only game in town." Was I sounding a little too self-effacing? I didn't want pity—but what *did* I want?

"Don't say that. Yes, I do like to dance, but not just with anyone. You don't see me going to clubs or anything to dance, do you?" She immediately answered her own question with, "No, you don't."

Did I detect a little anger? Or was it frustration? Katie had become somewhat agitated—there was tension in her movement, in her body that I held so closely. The *bandoneón* now challenged the violin—a duel in duet.

"I dance with you, because I want to be with you, and because... it pleases me," she said simply.

At this point, I could feel a contraction, as though Katie's body had shrunk, becoming more supple in my arms. The music became softer; now the violins took the melody to another level.

"So...why do you spend time with Josh?" Was I thrusting my argument into the heart of the issue, at whatever it was I seemed to desire? Why change the mood? We were going somewhere, but I couldn't stay. In the background, a piano was heard trying to overshadow the violin in its quest for the *bandoneón*.

"Well, for one thing...oh, I don't know...because..."

Suddenly a yearning *bandoneón* spoke, the violin waiting... How was it possible to reason? But perhaps *reasoning* wasn't what was called for. I had made my point. The piano sounded out the strains of fleeting feelings, the violin answering its own melancholic notes. Katie hadn't been able to give me her reasons for dating the likes of Josh, or maybe it was because she didn't want to.

"I shouldn't have told you Josh is jealous." Katie shifted her weight as I led her to the cross, placing her left foot firmly in back of her right. "Actually, he doesn't come right out and say, 'I'm jealous. I want you to stop dancing—or whatever it is you do with Aaron.' It's not his way—not that I know what his 'way' is. No, it's...well, he becomes silent whenever your name comes up—and it comes up often, I can tell you. So his silences are noticeable, and when I ask him why he's silent, he changes the subject, like he doesn't want to talk about what's bothering him."

Bandoneón, violin and piano now played in trio, of feelings felt but not expressed.

"Katie, if you know that mentioning my name bothers Josh, why mention it?" I thought that logical.

"Oh, sweetie, you don't understand women, thinking like you do."

That got me wondering if maybe she was right. Maybe I *didn't* understand women at all.

"I'm not using you to provoke Josh, it's not that—and in any case, I would never do a thing like that." At this point, Katie moved her hand from my left shoulder, guiding it upward to entangle her fingers within the hair at the back of my head. "No, it's not that, not that at all. It's...well...it's that it gives me pleasure talking about you; you must realize that. You do, don't you?"

"Recalling Sun Tzu, the supreme art of war is to subdue the enemy without fighting. I would call upon my shored-up patience—a necessity in battle."

The *bandoneón* picked up the theme...and carried it beyond the stars and the heavens, to places unknown.

What could I say? Any protest on my part would appear immodest, and while I don't mind tooting my own horn on occasion, it sounds much, much better hearing Katie toot it for me. The *bandoneón* joined the violin, their melodies more intense with each note played. Their music ached with the feeling of unanswered passion, of intense longing, thirsting to be quenched...its natural finale.

We danced in silence, with only the *bandoneón*, violin and piano for companions. I held her close, Katie allowing me to use my body as a sort of protective cloak around her. The melody remained plaintive, speaking of longing, an aching feeling...somewhere.

"You know, Josh is stubborn. You wouldn't believe how utterly obstinate he can be."

Should I have remarked that such a trait is an indicator of

immaturity, perhaps even of insecurity?

"You know, Katie, Josh is young, and while he lives in the most 'sophisticated' city in the world, not every New Yorker is worldly. Is that important to you?"

"Yes and no; it depends. He's also headstrong over the pettiest things, like the music we listen to. When we're together he only wants to listen to East Coast swing—whatever that is. He won't listen to tango, and forget about classical music."

"Have you tried to introduce him to what you like?"

"I've put on some of the tango music you've given me, and he asks if I could play something else. You know how much I enjoy Beethoven, especially the piano sonatas. Well, forget about that too."

We continued to meander around the floor, slowly, reflecting Katie's mood.

"He's so bullheaded. He won't compromise, always wanting it his way."

"Maybe no one has taken an interest in forming his tastes, to something more elevated...like Beethoven? Give him time."

It's not that I liked or disliked Josh. Perhaps I should take a page from Maugham's story and challenge him to a duel. We were at the cross, always a good place to think, to plan the next move or sequence.

"You're right, but youth—and I categorize Josh as such, because, well, he looks so young—can be stiff-necked, pig-headed and unyielding. I don't know if I want him to come up for Valentine's Day."

The music stopped—and so did our dancing. For the music, it was a change of tangos; for me, a jolt. *Valentine's Day! So soon?* "Has Josh mentioned that he intends to return for Valentine's Day?"

"Yes. He said he wants to spend it with me, just me."

I considered leading a *molinete*, but then thought, *Why?* "What about the kids?" But, on second thought, *Why not?*

"Oh, they'll be with their father."

"Well, what is it that you object to then, I mean about Josh's visit?" I was trying to do a *lápiz*, but the *bandoneón* began a yearning motif that our feet followed, languidly.

"I'm not sure I want to spend that holiday with him. It's not that I don't enjoy his company—in spite of his rigidity. It's, just, well, his personality lacks...depth."

Now we were getting somewhere—at least I thought we were as I kicked out a gancho.

"I feel like I'm treading water when I'm with him. I don't know, maybe I'm just being..."

"You're being honest with yourself." I felt Katie gancho through my legs as I turned her, placing my arms around her waist. "Why not let him come and spend the holiday with you? It will give you more time to make a decision."

"Perhaps I haven't been clear about what I mean." Katie was

now performing back *boléos*. "You see, to some people, Valentine's Day is the day for lovers." I felt Katie move closer—to close our embrace—Pugliese receding. "It's got romantic connotations and all that."

On the *bandoneón*, notes were tripling, tumbling. "If I let Josh come up, he may get the wrong impression, you know, of my feelings towards him, and I don't want to lead him on. I think if I encourage him by saying okay to spending that day with him, knowing the way he may feel about it being Valentine's Day, you know, it might lead him to think that I have feelings for him. You know what I mean?"

I went into cross-basic, holding Katie so that she could perform a front *boléo* from the side position—which she did to perfection.

"You may be right, but why not tell Josh how you feel about Valentine's Day...that, to you, it isn't a big deal. Don't say it like that, of course; make it sound, well, less like a potential put-down. Then he won't be misled. If he misinterprets your feelings about the two of you spending Valentine's Day together, then that's his problem, isn't it? Not yours."

"You're right. I know that's what I should do—and I'll do it. I feel better, but it's strange. None of my friends like Josh...and neither do the kids." At that moment, the piano was playing against the orchestra, as though they were arguing. I felt a genuine sense of sympathy for Josh. He had probably never met someone like Katie before. The violins now joined the *bandoneón*, *juntos*, and we continued our way to the cross.

"What is it they don't like? I mean, I've only met Josh twice, so don't count me, because I'll always play devil's advocate."

"The kids don't find him fun, or even interesting. Maybe it's because he hasn't been too interested in *them*."

"I'm surprised Willie and Josh haven't hit it off...they're both into history. It's one of the subjects Josh teaches, and Willie reads historical books all the time." I could hear the voice of Carlos Gardel in the mournful song of the *bandoneón*.

"That's what I'm saying. Josh teaches American history, and doesn't appear to be interested in any *other* history. Willie reads all kinds of history, like the Churchill books you gave him, not just the history of *this* country."

"Yeah, Willie and I had an interesting discussion about Catherine the Great. He was fascinated that an obscure German princess could take over a country like Russia and turn it into a world power."

The violin picked up the melody and brought the notes to a new height.

"You see! You and Willie have more in common. That's what kids want, someone who takes an interest in what *they're* interested in, and Josh doesn't...like how he won't take an interest in the music *I* like."

I could hear the *bandoneón* once more arguing with the violin, creating a moment of dissonance.

"My friends think Josh is just too young and self-centered. But your opinion...it means more to me than all the others, and I don't think you like Josh all that much." Katie looked at me in such a shy manner, tilting her head so that her expression, especially her eyes, seemed to make a circle, like a *lápiz*, until they were glancing up at me in a hide-and-seek fashion: almost a challenge—but a coquettish one. The violin had stolen the melody and was turning the tango into a milonga dance, which I never enjoyed—so I stopped.

"I would never suggest telling you what to do; I just don't want you to make a mistake. But if you must make one, let it be a minor one, one not too difficult to overcome and forget."

We began dancing again as the *bandoneón* had overtaken the violin, its tone doleful. I could feel Katie's body moving gently, like velvet. To her, dancing and movement expressed her moods, her emotions. I knew at that moment she was being reflective; through her body, I could almost *feel* her thoughts. I wondered if I was as transparent to her. Could Katie feel *my* thoughts, *my* emotions? I didn't quite say that, in my opinion, no one would be good enough for her—but I came close. If Josh showed up for Valentine's Day, it might give him sufficient rope to hang himself—and I wouldn't have to challenge him to a duel.

***

"Well, I had an interesting experience," Katie announced as we embraced the following Tuesday. When, during the past year that I'd known Katie, had she *not* had an interesting experience? And when had she not told me about it, *all* about it—the gory details, far more details than I cared to know, yet also needed to know, to satisfy my innate curiosity, my desire to hear all about her and her life apart from me?

"At my modern dance class, this guy..." *I knew it, I knew it. It had to be...yet, I could be wrong.* "...asked me out for coffee."

And? I probed with my eyes.

"I told him I couldn't—not then, as I was meeting you—but we had a chat. That's why I'm a bit late." *And?* "He actually asked if he might take me out." *Sweet, how old-fashioned...the dog!* "I told him I was already dating somebody." *Good. Let it stay that way.* "Then he asked if we could just have a coffee, from time to time. You know, no big deal, no heavy stuff." *I could just see it: the guy panting over a latte, drooling over his Danish, slobbering over his words.* "I told him, 'Sure, why not?' After all, I'm not committed to Josh—not at this point, anyway."

I looked at Katie. Here she was, not two months after telling me she needed a breather, that entanglements would be shelved. Well, I guess entanglements these days have a very short shelf life. What happened to just dating—without the heavy breathing, the messy involvements, the need to be at home when *he* calls, playing the field and that sort of thing?

We started dancing—a waltz—but Katie was so wrapped up in her tale that she lost her form.

"Katie, this is not a Viennese waltz. I think you watch *Dancing with the Stars* too much. Look at me...that's right. Now pretend we're just tangoing, none of that head held high and away business...and, come closer...yes, close embrace. I want to feel your body against mine... Yes, like that... What's this guy's name? You haven't mentioned his name." My voice revealed a little testiness.

"Ernie; his name is Ernie."

"And Ernie, what does he do—aside from taking modern dance classes?" Nosy, to the point, blunt, inquisitive—whatever it's called. I was being overbearing as well. "That's right, a little lilting, but keep the rhythm...better. Now I'm going into cross-basic." Wow, Katie did a front *boléo*, with her left leg as I held her against my right shoulder without my leading it.

"Ernie's a contractor. He has his own company...in Belvidere, I think. I don't know that much about him. We've only just talked—and that was only for a few minutes." Katie did a pirouette—a tango pirouette—again without being led. I wondered what else she was doing without me leading her. I could see it all: Ernie's in, Josh is out. Musical lovers, a new game for adults. But I didn't seem to be the one calling the tune. I looked at Katie again. How could I be upset? All she was doing was what came naturally—to her—what came naturally to all of us. To some, it came more easily than to the rest, but it's all there, in our genes, ready to pop out when needed—or led.

"What do you think will happen?" As if I had to ask such an obvious question.

"Well, I'm not sure..."

Come on, Katie, don't play games—not with me. I know you know, and I know you know that I know you're going to tell me. So?

"Josh...well, he's unsophisticated—and he's young, too."

The music faded—and so did Josh's prospects.

"How old is Ernie?"

"In his thirties..."

"So is—was—Josh."

"True, true. But Ernie's a more *mature* thirtyish."

That was rationalization, pure rationalization. I know. I was trained as an economist, and if there's any group of people that knows how to exploit the art of rationalization, it's us economists. If the economy is getting too hot, we rationalize it as cooling off; and if the economy is in a downturn, we rationalize it into an expansion. I could rationalize anything into the right and proper thing. With Katie, it was called hormonal rationalization. Did Freud ever think of that?

"Okay. Ernie's more mature. But why dump Josh—unless he's not a long-term prospect?" Here I go, always thinking like an economist: maximizing at the margin, converting everything, including emotions, feelings and thoughts, into quantifiable variables.

"Josh is sweet, he really is, in spite of his stubbornness. I've told you he's obdurate, unbending..." *I did remember an extraordinary vocabulary used to describe the fellow.* "...he's sweet and kinda cute. Well, you've met him. I just think I need someone more...well, more...you know what I mean."

The waltz turned into a slow tango, one in which you move, just move, one step at a time, without thinking, or preparing. A time to be in the moment. That was Katie. She could be so articulate at times, and so obscure at others. Practical—like when she's buying a new car or refinancing her mortgage—and, then impractical—like now. Not that I regarded choosing between Josh and Ernie as an exercise in practicality. Then again, maybe it was and I hadn't recognized it—yet.

"This guy, Ernie, does he have any attachments?" Now I was making him sound like an email.

"No, none that I know of. I only just met him, remember?"

How could I forget? "So, he's not married?"

"Nope, nor has he ever been."

Thirtyish and never married? My suspicions reared their ugly—or maybe they were really attractive—heads. I knew we lived in Northern Vermont where prospects were slim pickings, but even the ugliest, most homely, the stupidest found someone, usually before they were out of junior high. How had Ernie managed to avoid the inevitable Vermont experience? Perhaps he was craftier than I thought. Perhaps Ernie was smart. What a shocker that would be. But was he clever? I knew many smart people—but few were clever. And, I knew a few clever people—and most were not smart. To be both—smart *and* clever—that was the winning combination, the duo that I needed to build my forces for combat.

"I presume then that he doesn't have children?" Up here, you could never take that for granted. People reproduce like rabbits—and marriage wasn't a precondition, nor an obstacle.

"No—no children. At least I don't believe so. He didn't speak of any. I told him about mine, and he didn't admit to any of his own. But I imagine I'll hear more about his private life—if I see more of him, that is."

I was sure, too. Knowing Katie, I would be the first to be told as well. That was my role—at the moment. I needed to be more careful—less critical, less judgmental, more generous—to leave the corridor to my cunning open and clear of impediments. I should take a page from my mother's book of wisdom: *Aaron, it doesn't cost you a penny to let praise fall upon your enemies.*

Thanks, Mom. I'll remember.

"Let's dance, shall we?" Katie suggested as she rested in my embrace. Wasn't that what we had *been* doing? I couldn't believe we had spent all this time talking and not dancing—except for a desultory attempt at waltzing.

Sun Tzu advised that strategy without tactics is the slowest route to victory, but tactics without strategy is the noise before defeat. I needed any and all information so that I could form my plan, to marshal all my forces, for I had yet to discover Ernie's vulnerabilities...

***

It had been more than a week since I learned about Ernie. Josh didn't come up for Valentine's Day; that much I'd been spared. Since then, I had learned more about her new friend.

"Ernie's an excavator."

Katie told me this as were trying a new routine, using *nuevo tango* music—Piazzolla-style—to take us deeper into the inner voice of the dance. "He digs foundations, you know, for homes and such..." I held Katie back a little longer than I usually do as the music—being *nuevo*—called for a more modern interpretation. "But he doesn't pour the cement." I think I held her just a tad too long, for Katie began leaning back against my right arm. "He grades roads..." I brought her back, placing my right foot against hers, in preparation for a morida. "And driveways..." Holding her, I moved my left foot and, bending my knee inward, pressed my right one against hers, to slide *her* right foot over to meet our left feet. "But he doesn't maintain them." I stepped back, holding Katie in place. "Occasionally he does carpentry..." Katie stepped forward, and before I could take a breath, did a front *boléo*—unled. "And that's how he built his own house." I was so proud of her. "Ernie's handy..." We then stepped together, but not to go to the cross. "If you need a carpenter or someone to excavate the foundation of the house you plan to build..." I led her to step around me so that I could *sacada* her trailing foot. "...or grade your driveway. Anyway, Ernie's nice; he's polite."

I learned a lot about Ernie, about as much as I truly wanted to know, information that I might be able to use later—when it was needed to destroy Mr. Nice Guy in battle.

***

"Hi. Sorry for disturbing you, but I just *had to* call."

"You can call me anytime, you know that."

"I know, but you might have been immersed in something and not want to be disturbed... Anyway, what I wanted to tell you was that I've told Josh." There was a pause; not a "catching your breath" pause; not an "I have to go to the bathroom" pause; not a "the baby's in the bathtub drowning" pause; not a "we've been disconnected" pause. Silence.

"Katie, are you still there?"

"Yeah. I was just collecting eggs from my chickens. I forgot to tell you I was in the chicken coop." Ah. It was *that* kind of pause. "Like I was saying, I've told Josh."

"What? Katie, what have you told Josh?" My heart started racing, pumping: *boom...boom...boom*, like that. It always did when I felt victory was in my grasp. I thought I knew what Katie had told Josh, but I wanted Katie to tell me, not for me to second-guess her.

"I broke up with him. I told Josh that it's over between us."

"I needed to be more careful—less critical, less judgmental, more generous—to leave the corridor to my cunning open and clear of impediments. I should take a page from my mother's book of wisdom: Aaron, it doesn't cost you a penny to let praise fall upon your enemies."

My heart settled down: *ka-boom...ka-boom...ka-boom*. I knew this was coming, ever since New Year's Eve. Not for any reason, really—and I was still smarting over Katie's comment that I didn't understand women. Now I liked Josh, perhaps because he was no longer a threat, perhaps only a teaser along the way.

"I thought you would—once you met Ernie, I mean." What should I have told her, that it takes more than sex to keep a long-distance affair aflame? Why be so crass—insightful as it might be?

"It wasn't only Ernie that inspired me to do it. I've told you how I felt about Josh." *Yeah, but I wasn't about to go through the litany of adjectives we'd used to describe him.* "He was cute..." *Cute?* Josh was handsome...but I didn't remind her. "And sweet, in a way, but I need more than that."

And you can get it with Ernie? But I didn't say that either; I could practice restraint—on occasion.

"You know..." here Katie's voice became somewhat pensive. "It wasn't a true relationship. I mean, between Josh and me. It was an interlude."

I think, at that moment, I realized that my education was just beginning, and here I thought for years that earning a doctorate was the highest level. Perhaps an "interlude" was part of a post-graduate course, one called Understanding Women, that fate was teaching me in real time.

"I know that you were only seeing Josh since before Christmas, but I thought it had *some* depth to it, or was I mistaken?" Bitchy; subtle, but bitchy.

"Sweetie, how can you call dating a guy for less than three months a relationship? It isn't; it's an interlude, that's all. Relationships have to last at *least* six months, otherwise they can't be classified as such." Katie was getting deeper into her subject—and I was all ears. "What Josh and I had, well, it only began in December. That's less than three months. So it was an interlude—a period between relationships. You see the difference, don't you?"

Of course, of course. It was simple—only I didn't quite grasp the logic behind Katie's argument. But what did I know? I knew how to dance Argentine tango. I knew how to hold a woman in an embrace and lead her to dance all the moves I'd taught her. I knew how to laugh with her, and cry with her, and be there for her. I could share a latte with her after having our ears pierced. I could bring milongas to my restaurant. I could criticize her choice of men, and back up my opinions with rationale. I could wait patiently while a string of suitors filed through her life, and listen—at times impatiently—while she sang their praises. I could put my feelings in winter storage so that she could make her own decisions. I knew how to do all those things— but I couldn't grasp the logic of Katie's argument. I must have sounded so dated and conservative. The next thing she'll accuse me of is being a Republican. I must find a course on how to appear to be more liberal and less archaic.

"You're right. I see your point. It's not that I want to make a pitch on Josh's behalf, but he has—had—the looks, he's educated, holds down a respectable job, isn't married or attached..."

"Yes, but..."

"He's young, meaning he's still developing his interests. And, yes, he might be stubborn, as you say, but that could indicate that he stands up for what he believes in..."

"Yes, but..."

"And, he dances swing, East Coast-style, and doesn't appear to be interested in learning tango..."

"Yes, but..."

"When will you see Ernie again?"

"Actually tonight. Since my ex has the kids, I thought inviting Ernie over here would be perfect."

Yeah, right; perfect for who? It was amazing to me how easily one lover slips in, as the one who's in, slips out—seamlessly. Just as I was beginning to set my sights on knocking Josh off the pedestal he never quite managed to ascend, he's told to get lost. I was disappointed. After all, I had expended some energy in undermining his quest. Maybe my exertions hadn't been in vain. Perhaps they just might have contributed to his disappearing act. I hate to shoot my bolt and not see the results, not see it hitting some target.

In my mind, we danced. We are somewhere—it doesn't matter where—and Katie has on her tights and her jersey top, and a Mona Lisa smile that always causes me to stop—and think. I hold her in my arms, imagining it is "our" Tuesday. Only a *bandoneón* plays as we move slowly, together. *Juntos*.

"A penny for your thoughts," I say in this sweet fantasy.

"Only a penny?" she replies.

"Okay, how about a dime?"

"Now you're talking."

I take out a dime...and place it securely behind her ear.

"This is what I really want..." she says. "Just you...and me...and..."

"Is there something else?"

"Perhaps the kids...at home...waiting."

We continue, not really tangoing, just being...together.

What could I do? No matter what happened, Katie would always be Katie. When we danced—even in my imagination—I forgot everything else in our lives. I only thought—and felt—the dance...and Katie. She had contributed so much to the enjoyment of my life—and dancing the tango—I would have forgiven her everything. If there were anything to forgive, that is.

1970

James Stuart Nolte

So I Jameson/Oberon, along with my friend, Dev/Puck, talked the fairies and sprites of our high school play into going as a group to see a screening of *Yellow Submarine* and we gathered on the wire at about seven, ready to fly south, a flock of teenaged birds whose plan it was to get blasted on LSD and drive in two yellow Volkswagen Beetles to see The Beatles movie. Puck had the acid, tiny purple pills in a little prescription drug envelope. He handed it around and they all peeped in. There were fifteen imps and only fourteen pills. What to do? Laying in a neat and tidy pile in the trash on the floor of his dub-dub, were some schoolbooks. Dev tore a page out of his civics textbook, folded it into squares, dropped the pills in and, using a hammer, pounded the little darlings into powder. He then poured the powder out onto a hand mirror and made fifteen more or less equal lines while we all rolled up dollar bills and then proceeded sniffing up each allotment in turn. This was not a standard pharmacological method for apportioning dosages. But everybody stood around smoking joints and sharing beers, waiting to see which ones of us got the bullets.

As time went along, it turned out everyone was at least wounded. Excitement was brewing in the group like a thick smoke around a fire that only needed air to burst into flames. Every patterned fabric was vibrating. Blue jean suddenly became an exotic blue ocean of possibilities as it lay in the green, green suburban grass and the green, green trees started to breathe hard in the darkening blue, blue sky, and the trees whispered amongst themselves about the colorful clothes of these children and about how, soon, the trees themselves would change into similarly-patterned and veined colors and blow off into the four winds.

Excited to be off. We were definitely _off_. Words jumped out of mouths in a jumble. I touched and jostled friends as if they were my favorite stuffed toys come alive. We loved each other so much. All sound was being subtly interrupted and modulated by a frantic short circuit in our ears. The universe and everything in it was a gift we all wanted. It was time to go.

***

It is very difficult to keep a car on the road with all the general distractions offered by a living universe. One is continually tempted to turn the wheel and follow some cosmological or visual disruption to its conclusion. But there _is_ a reality, and a basic tenet in this situation is that those things which were real, and those things I saw now, were different. The trick is to remember what you used to do with the normal stuff. It takes real mental courage to be a driver on an untamed road just let out of its corral. So I assiduously followed the road that I knew, no matter where it tried to go now that it had been freed. If it turned left when it used to go right, I took the courage to bear right where it used to go instead of veering left where it wanted. Doing this tames the road. The car sort of noses the road into place ahead of it. Now and then, it tried to buck me off and the people in back bounced up and down in time to broken shocks and worn springs, making the car seem to be curious about, first, what was on one side of the road, and then, suddenly, what was on the _other_ side.

To any outside observer, the car appeared to be sniffing along the gutters and shaking its head saying, like a private in battle led by an incompetent sergeant, "Sir, we are _never_ going to make it." There were times when the vehicle seemed to leave the road surface altogether. We were going at an unknown speed because my vision was too distorted to read the speedometer. So, our two Bugs flew along back-country ways, down into the ravines and up over the rills and hills. I understood not a word of what the guy on the radio station was saying, although later I realized it was somebody talking in the back seat.

Puck flew past me and raced out ahead. He was carrying a couple of stolen road construction flashers and his car pulsed with an inner yellow light. When we saw them last, they were rounding a corner on two wheels, and two or three people were hanging half-naked out of the sunroof. Then I discovered why we were passed so fleetly: my car had come out of gear, inadvertently rolling to a stop. From then on, I tried to keep the white line in the speedometer about in the middle as I followed the leader. Soon, rounding another corner, we saw a marvelous sight. A spaceship with flashing red and blue lights had pulled Puck over.

"...we gathered on the wire at about seven, ready to fly south, a flock of teen-aged birds whose plan it was to get blasted on LSD and drive in two yellow Volkswagen Beetles to see The Beatles movie."

By all accounts, everyone in the car was very cool. They had been fooled often enough by volunteer firemen cars and their lights to have practiced abandoning shit. *Ditch the dope.* Roll down the window. Drive long enough to clear the air. Light cigarettes. The girls arrange themselves according to a picture of cuteness. The policeman walks up, the driver of the car reads his lines. The audience eats its heart out hearing Puck say clearly and cheerfully, "Hi Mr. Bummer."

The message here is that drugs will make you do and say anything, thought the audience, now critics about to go down the tube with the play.

"Hi Dev," said the policeman. He knew Dev. He knew Dev's dad. His name really was Mr. Bummer. The chorus didn't know this. This was classical tragedy to them, theater where you know the ending.

But Patrolman Bummer liked Dev. There were a couple of people in the front seat he didn't like. But he liked Dev. Dev was just good, clean, all-American fun.

"Um, Dev," the officer began in an avuncular way, "where did you get those works lights, fella?"

"Aah jeez, Mr. Bummer. My dad's had those around for a long time."

"You know, Dev, a couple of those blockades turned up by Yellow Creek Road last week..."

Dev smiled and replied, "Mr. Bummer, I think they'll probably turn up again."

And Officer Bummer said, "Fine. I'll let you go now. Say hi to your mom and dad for me."

"Sure thing, Mr. Bummer."

"And one more thing, Dev: it's not safe to drive at night with sunglasses on."

Dev smiled and agreed, "Yes, Mr. Bummer."

"That motherfucker's name is Bummer?" My sister, Aleah/Titania, squeaked hilariously, as they pulled off the berm and back onto the road. "Oh, far out!" she moaned in ecstasy, adding, "A real bummer." And everybody turned into pink balloons filled with laughter that floated away into a purple sky.

Meanwhile, our car passed this scene, an obvious bust of headline proportions, and as we witnessed the strobing, incandescent event, we knew that our castmates' lives, once so free, would, from now on, become formalized in courts of law. In my car, our cousin, Mary/Cobweb, freaked and puked out the window. Oh well.

After a brief silent prayer, we philosophically continued down the road smoking dope and singing, "We all live in a yellow submarine, a yellow submarine, yellow submarine." And the repetition was important. Rose/Mustardseed began to faint, probably from smoke inhalation because the Volkswagen was like a huge bong chamber on wheels, but when she tried to open a window, someone said, "Hey man, don't let the air out or we'll drown, 'cause..." And we all started up again: "We all live in a yellow submarine, a yellow submarine, yellow submarine."

We had zeroed in on the theater parking lot, where, to our surprise and delight, a reincarnated Dev pulled up in his Bug, opened the doors and out poured all the sprites and fairies in a semi-liquid state. A man, with a little girl in tow, on their way to the theater, passed the tangled group and asked how they could get so many people in a Volkswagen. "Smoke and mirrors, man, smoke and mirrors." And everyone thought that was hilarious.

POETRY

How to Sulk Effectively When You Can't Get Your Way

Antonia Alexandra Klimenko

1

Feel sorry for yourself
Put on a sad face
Dress in fatigues
Be hard to please
Tell them you're fine
sniff sniff never better
Talk about the weather
Be ambiguous unclear and indirect
SHOW them you're upset
Tell them nothing
they might otherwise on their own suspect

2

Know your target
(It's always the one who cares)
Even the score   wage a cold war
Gently reject and refuse them   confuse them
Make them regret
how you were wronged
how your needs weren't met
Be your own work of fiction
a living contradiction
the center of their attention
at the far end of the couch
buried in your book
If you're standing   just crouch

3

Be highly and visibly invisible
Appear disappear
Make them fear the end is near

Collapse relapse
Be a tower of Jell-O a puddle of drool
Let your shoulders hunch sag
Never nag   Above all be cool
Why shout when you can pout lie about
A moan every now and then   can't hurt
Just Sighhhhhhhhhhhh when in doubt

4

Strategize
improvise
Neglect the call of lust
Dishes in the sink
but don't forget to dust
Let your silence do the talking
facial expressions impressions depression
use your eyes
Downcast sullen vacant unglued
Make like a willow   weep into your pillow
Woe is me   am i blue

5

Always leave the door open   just a crack
so you're ever on display
flat on your back
A shared misery can take hours
or drag on for days
But surely they'll surrender
You have your ways
And until then…finally

6

Just remember
Don't speak play hide and seek refuse to eat
stock up on snacks   dress all in black

Copy paste or download
Follow me for future hacks.

My Garments Languish

Dale Champlin

shimmying from the banister
  drifting down twenty-three steps
    to our home's midriff

landing above the knees
  It's not for nothing,
    this accumulation

I can't give my skirts,
  my tights, my scarves
    up for lost

I refuse to say *au revoir*
  although at some point
    I may be forced to relinquish

the way they crush my nipples
  brush my thighs
    fill observers with sighs

and *oh mys!*
  I might be mistaken
    for a lady of some sort

Up on the third floor
  my dresses define
    the epitome of high fashion

some adorn
  one or more forlorn
    a few never worn

sanctimonious tomfoolery
  oh là là hoopla or bilk
    velvet, denim and silk

capricious—hardly sentient
   I can't give them up
      any more than I can

you   or you   or you
   though at some point
      I will be forced to

abandon their un-
   closeted wildness
      Dear spectator

your love pierces me
   like a needle
      through gauze

yet, to my regret
   I have spent
      my whole life

      pinked
     stitched
    trimmed
  cut from whole cloth
   and hemmed in

What Enters the Locked Room

Mary Birnbaum

The universe is about to fall on the house.
Biblical plagues.
Or a giant tree of life, planetary trunk,
leaves sharp as pterodactyl wings.

A storm of angels will rocket from heaven.
Fear always finds anger.
What a loneliness shudders in the cosmic wind
beyond the lovely stars.

And what's hiding in the voices digging
for respect in your soul?
Unending night can't be ignored, immensity
sneaks in through keyholes.

The sun insinuates a movie onto a wall.
In the quick frame,
liquid smoke dissipates in light. Stripped trees
are miming the rising wind.

How Vision Is Freed

Mary Birnbaum

God assigned Hieronymus Bosch
his meticulous detail, appalling insight,
an iridescence precise as a fly,
brief car in distance,
passing through a gap
between tiny buildings.

Through the moonlight's haze on the lens,
through gaps of a mask's webbing,
I see a magnified insect,
beaked, its tail flowing,
feathered, a bird with mail
forged from chains of metallic script.

I feel its Latin needle rip my throat,
its thin singing beyond hearing.
In dream, any attempt at answer is futile.
Hope is a splinter of yearning.
I see God's signal. Heaven's
weird hosts winging.

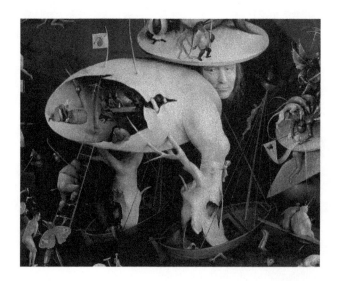

Song of the Winged Witch

Mary Birnbaum

No moon, but the air hums clear,
a tuning fork. Pines hush green strings,
oaks vibrate into frozen roots.
My head spirals, a bush sighs,
paws pad through gentle snow.
I note fox, weasel, lynx.
I map prey they've missed,
a squeak, a scuttle, susurrus
in buried leaves. I flex talons,
I rise from the hollow, hungering
for a heartbeat in shadow.

Bastille Day

Floyd Humphrey

I stood on the bridge, in the same spot
we stood last year. This time, however,
the night was a lot warmer.
Sadness, like cold water,
poured over me as I reminisced.

You wore a blue dress without any underwear
and I stood, in jealous protection, close to prevent
the wind, by chance, of showing what precious
jewel was hidden underneath.

There were a group of young men in kayaks
trying to row against the tide, do you remember?
We laughed at their foolish attempts
of getting nowhere fast.

I held you close as the night air brought
the chill of the river with it; I gave you my top.
We were happy, very happy, because all was new
and we were full of expectations.

Or so I thought! Shakespeare was right about
walking slowly, for fear of stumbling. Prince
advised one kiss at a time. But I was in a hurry
and overwhelmed you with my affection.

Now I see it is never wise to over-feed someone
who has been starved and malnourished.
Sure enough, this killed what would
have been a very happy future together.

One year later and I am standing
alone on a packed bridge.
The fireworks are as fantastic as ever.
Those around me *oooh!* and *aaah!* after each
explosion of light, then turn to each other and
exchange glances of acknowledged appreciation.
I have no one with whom to exchange such glances.
I wonder if you ever think about that night or, just

like each spent firework, the memories have
instantly disappeared without a trace.

I can't help thinking that this display was like our
relationship, lots of dazzling lights, big finale,
then nothing!
With the crowd, I slowly made my lonely way back home.

Blood Lines

Floyd Humphrey

What is seen and lived by children
mark them throughout their lives.
The anxieties and worries never leave,
they become multiplied, clouding their vision,
clouding and impairing their judgement,
preventing them from breaking free from
the difficult thoughts inside their head.

When it is their turn to face these problems,
panic and fear overwhelm them.
They hate themselves, they hate their lives,
they even hate those they are meant to love.
Looking in the mirror reflects the burdens of
those who bully and intimidate them, and
there is no escape from the hell in which they live.

So, the blood lines are their only way of saying,
"Help me please!" And it becomes a ritual,
then a victorious defeat against an invisible enemy,
as invisible as the battle scars hidden from others.
What council can we give so that they can understand
the important role they play in the lives of others
so that no more blood lines can be drawn?

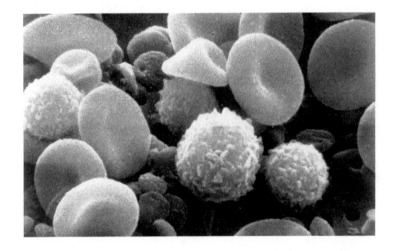

Education

Floyd Humphrey

The bell
rings the cruel reminder that fun is over,
and the children are forced to forget playful
joy and laughter—
to forget the very emotions which differentiates
them from adults—
to succumb to a learning process
which favours finishing the syllabus,
instead of nourishing the mind.
Space to run and play and discover
is exchanged for hours of immobility
in confinement,
often inadequately heated,
often inadequately ventilated.
Time, from an emotionless
face,
d
r
i
p
s,

d
r
i
p
s,

d
r
i
p
s.

They drown in the boredom of their captors,
waiting to be released by the very thing
which put them there,
The bell!

There's A Party On Witch Meadow Road

Charlie Robert

Snow.
Wipers.
Blow.
Vipers.
Watch Out For
Yesterday's Snipers.
There's A Wolf
At The Door.
With A Blade
At His Neck.
There's The Tired
And The Poor.
Blank Check.
Lots Of Likes
Lucky Strikes
Keep Your Head
In The Game.
Downshift.
Blue Flame.
Party Room.
Blow Your Top.
Mount Doom.
Lollipop.
Dead Aunts.
On Parade.
Your Pants.
Gatorade.
Your Chance.
Passed You By.
Kind Words.
Lullaby.
You're Making
Us Cry So
Don't Forget
To Have Your Fun.
Don't Forget

Your Killer Gun.
Don't Forget
Tupac Your Load.
Don't Forget.
They Changed The Code.
There's A Party
On Witch Meadow Road.
Bring Your Jack.
Love Shack.

Greta's Closet

Charlie Robert

Ancient Furs.
Mink And Stoat.
Moth Balls
In Metal Cans.
Secrets.
Plans.
Pictures.
Pledges.
Curled At
The Edges.
Scattered
Like Lies.
Dead Flies.
Waiting
For Heirs
To Discard Them.
Jewels.
Made Of
Glass.
Gold.
Brass.
Mirrors.
Dust.
Yesterday's Lust.
Yesterday's Gone.
In God We Rust.
Moth Balls.
In Metal Cans.
Pills.
Plans.

Knock Knock.
Button Lock.

The Intimate Friend

John Bradley

Look. His back has turned, turned upon us all.
There's no end to the denials of an intimate friend.
Denying his erotic glass of wine, his amorous baguette.

While his back has turned, I can say anything.
There's no end to the horniness of this intimate friend.
He kissed this glass of wine, this flirty baguette.

I can't stand it when he turns his back on me.
There's no end of what I dislike about my intimate friend.
His glass of cheap wine, his unfaithful baguette.

Yes, I'm talking behind his back, which can't talk back.
There's nothing else to say about our intimate friend.
So drink his lusty wine, devour his roving baguette.

Planetary Wobble

John Bradley

You feel frazzled, wearied, frayed, as if a blast of neutrinos
just blazed through your brain, each cell in your body flickering,
fluttering for a microsecond as the neutrinos sizzle and rattle
through, though it might have been something on the TV or radio
bleeding into something you ate, smeared with bleary shock,
blurry sigh, causing those tremors in the heart, these spells
of moodiness and unsteadiness, which can result, as we all know,
in subterranean shifting and lifting, then planetary wobble,
and everyone knows what that does to the intestinal tract, so—
feeling a bit dizzy, you lean against the wall, the window
frame, back of the nearest chair, trying to slow your in—and out—
breaths, looking for a soft place to land so you can tell whoever
happens to be surveilling you from the nearest satellite:
*Who? Me? Why I'm just testing the international gravitational
settings in case some poor dope, you know, gets dingy or something
and tumbles off the edge of this indigestible world.*

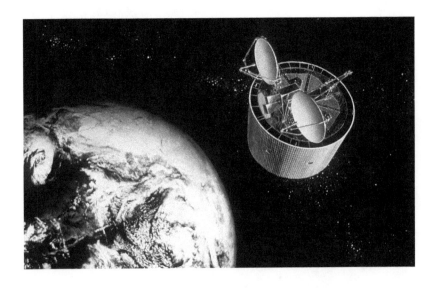

Sunday Driver

Mark Dunbar

The strip malls are endless,
false summits stretching out one
after the other, but we keep driving,
determined to escape the brand control.
The rumor is that you just keep going
until the parking lots turn to soil
that runs right to the edge of the road,
that you can walk in damp clay
glomming onto your feet as if
it had found something kindred,
that you can sink your hands into the warmth
of it like coarse ground coffee,
and the stain will be like a birthmark
and a ticket back into to that great room
that dawn makes of the night,
that room where your heart beats
Not Not Not
a vestige of,
not the exile's prayer,
not the lost cadence
haunting your dreams.

The Visit

Mark Dunbar

Beside the driveway to the mental home where
they've got my brother,
keen purposeful faces truant from their
afflictions bow down
as if fallen from a height,
hands in earth like seeds
misstrewn, I would say,
but for him, but for myself.

Cut grass and rectangular flower beds,
red tulips in a row—
would-be hosannas that plead
for salvation instead.
They're streaked orange, yellow and purple,
bend long stems like bows.
"Parrot tulips," mother says.
"There's virus in the bulbs."

We look up and you're there,
unattended, a good sign, we think,
until we catch your frantic stare
and hear that it's the wrong day,
that we're fugitives
lest they take you away
again.

Tell me is it like a fever
those voices no one else hears?
Is it some twisted shade
that makes you a believer?
Suddenly when you speak, and after years
I remember the dream
that mysteriously bound us together.

Now I only wonder what they've got you on,
your motions slow, your speech

forced up slurred from some well.
We're in separate hells.

Spirited to the crafts building
behind the maintenance shed,
we stand like spies before the window
to view the art show.
There in black and white and red
your pottery shines like a vision,
perfect as a wing.

And like museum-goers
we stare and stare.

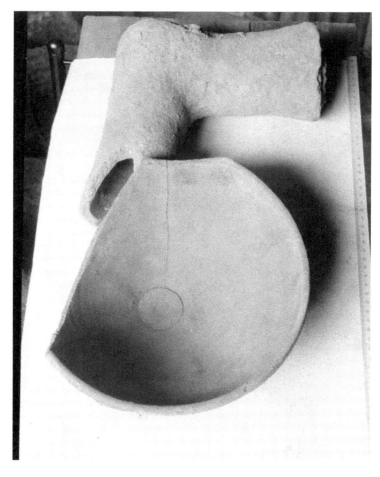

Ascent and Death

Heather Sager

For those who are out walking
one fine day and see a ladder
made of blue on the blue sky,
the rungs so clear they blend,
do you climb it?

For those stuck in a small town
the day the circus leaves,
the day the bookmobile shuts up,
do you meet someone who has stayed still
for decades, and, as evidenced
by their words, has just let
their mind die? If so,
how does that affect you?

Is it possible for hope to exist?
Are we all left alone as years pass?
Does yearning end? Perhaps
the best things live in the mind
and we are our own company.

Fire Survivors

Kevin Richard Kaiser

The jeweled horses survived
amusements, figures, contraptions,
bridles. Parents are watching children.
The carousel is watching parents.
The park is a concept: a dreamed place,
a vintage opportunity. A band plays
the better days of bucolic scenes.
Sister marches and waltzes, the gently-
worn feeling surrounded by an era
Disney dreamed was preserved.
Animated figures offset a gutted
façade, the priceless military destroying
the extraordinary craftsmanship
of the famous bench, lost in the parkland
background. Inspired, the organ cranks
and crashes the merry-go-round.

Field Notes from the Old Abandoned Zoo

Kevin Richard Kaiser

The animals facilitate a zoo.
The site is a find, a quiet location.
You may recognize the facilities
from the movie. You climb
a stairway winding the zoo
winding the hillside. The zoo
is a parkland, a Parkland. Eerie.

Cages have animals, the standard
helping: bear, lion, monkey. Pacing
like a zookeeper, you appear. The zoo
is lovely: the trail of pavement,
the picnic benches, the cave /
grotto / den outfitted with bars:
hard iron, rusted and creepy.

You climb. The old enclosures
seem small habitats. You find
coyotes. You have trouble.
You have feet. Enclosures
are a reminder. They give
a rare glimpse. Enclosures
are inspiring things.

You can picnic. Tiny enclosures
are sad. Just like parking. You find
a terrific watch. The old zoo
is out of the way: an outdated
animal-like animal. Read the field
notes. Parking is not hard.

Anti-Ode to Griffith J. Griffith

Kevin Richard Kaiser

> *Public parks are a safety valve of great cities*
> *and should be made accessible and attractive*
> *where neither race, creed nor color could be excluded.*
> -Col. Griffith

The story bought the land.
The property bought the form.

The eccentric donated a reputation:
"Colonel" leased ostrich feathers,
grabbed headlines, made a plain
obligation: sentiments are mental
revelations, and visitors must pass
the cemetery.

                     The masses
pass the bronze magnate. The man
had some friends. There is an exhibit
on scandalous escapades. A lavish
prison maintained a drunken park.
A paranoid shot unveiled his wife.

Home to his ego, the main entrance
to the observatory leaves some

happier,   cleaner.

High Power

Kevin Richard Kaiser

A neon coil is a home, alternating
currents. An enthusiastic experimenter

arcs therapies, electrotherapeutics
zapping our most tragic patients

for maximum wow: science on display.
From the loftiest neon vibrations,

electricity is free. The city is science.
Tesla discharges every hour on the hour.

A Modern Carousel

Kevin Richard Kaiser

Overlooking native automata,
the architecture is harrowing.
Hand-carved and hand-painted,
endangered peculiarities—
Komodo dragon, silverback gorilla,
poison dart frog, honey bee,
tapir, peninsular pronghorn,
double-wattled cassowary—
circle an imagination of conservation.
Nestled between princess pony
and mystical unicorn, the police
have friendly faces, welcoming.
The screenwriter, in desperate need,
can nestle between the dung beetles.

The Downward Spiral

Hugh Offor

Once as a younger man,
mid-crisis,
wounded,
fighting to understand
the incomprehensible,
my mother sat aside me
to give me a memory
of the 80s,
as a journalist,
on the beat,
of poverty, addictions and institutional neglect,
that classic suite of human suffering.

She said: "Hugh, be gentle, debased people, will do debased things,
simply because they feel debased."

Sound logic.
Circular,
yet well-rounded.
I ignored it,
as teenage sons are wont to do.

And yet as the calendar shed its leaves,
like tears, and we lost lovers
houses, jobs,
friends, family,
youth,
anything not nailed down,
                                    really,
I saw it again, and again,
this same circular motion.

I saw it in my friend's tired eyes,
as he smiled and clinked my pint—
the lights of the other world, spinning,
in the still room.

He was drinking again,
which meant he'd be taking pills again soon,
and we'd been here before,
and we both knew,

but I could change nothing,
and he was doing his best,
so what was the point in not smiling?

I tasted it too in the tears of another friend,
fallen in my mouth as they kissed me,
despite knowing I did not love them,
and I who let them,
despite being in love with another.

And again in my bedroom mirror,
struggling to recognize my own expression,
that indistinct outline of a man,
so warped by grief, shame,
laughing at his reflection,
unable to shake the distinct sensation
of being in free fall.

A leaf falling from the tree,
spirals.
The reason is mathematic:
Gravity plus resistance.

A person falling from the world,
spirals.
The reason is mathematic:
Gravity plus resistance.

Pulled down by the weight of the world,
it is so much to fight gravity,
and yet we do,
in tearful confessions,
apologies, dry spells,
fight to create a balance,
between self-destruction and preservation.

I see you,
tense bodies braced for an impact
that must surely be coming soon,
because you cannot fall forever.

This is our downward spiral.
the only question,
            is how to land.

The Irreparable

Hugh Offor

Kiss me not!
My spit is second-hand smoke,
An emotional carcinogen,
Ought be regulated,
The paperwork is in the pipeline
(or so I tell you),

But I am sick with confusion,
And with my garbled thoughts
Skewed reasons
Excuses and best intentions
I infect you too.

You are Narcissus' reflection,
Mirrored in my eyes.
Kiss me not,
I am not your bathroom mirror

You sigh to your friends
That I elude you,
Let me
be free from your desire.

Ask me write no promises,
Lest you come bearing wine,
Then all I assure is a slice.
Hold my hand while I carve it,
Lick the blood from my fingers,
Kiss my forrid,
Tell me I did good.

Such an uneasy thing it is to be loved,
Such a privilege to be desired.

But I forgive you,
For we are animals all,
Limp in the jaws of desire.

Saint Apocryphal

Richard Weaver

I have been called the last word by many who know no better. Better to say penultimate. It does have a ring. Some flare. Echoes of the Septuagint Bible to my mind. Most people, being ignorant, wrongly believe it's somehow an improvement on what is already ideal. Their poor minds have been programmed for drooling. Sad. But an audience is an audience. Admirers, not stalkers, are what we saints prefer. (Think of the Fall of Saint Patrick. A cautionary tale for all. I've heard rumors that newly anointed Saint Teresa has come under harsh review. By who, I can't say. Nor for what.) Reminds me: I owe Saint Parentheses some royalties. Years I've advocated for a union, one with higher standards. Not celestial ones. Realistic ones. It's hard enough living up to earthly laws and mores, especially these days, what with the internet and social media and all. Nothing escapes notice. What was once hidden, thought secret, invisible, is as easily had as a fortune cookie. You slip a fart in church, even a silent one, and there's a permanent mark beside your name. And CCTV. Every nose-pick caught on tape, digitized and cloud-stored until the clones come home. I'm not advocating a lowering of quality. Don't get me wrong here. I'm thinking we need to shake things up a bit with new blood, so to speak. Move past the fourteenth century mentality. Forward a century or two. Maybe three. Nothing too radical. Keep a safe distance from the twentieth. And never admit the twenty-first ever happened. I'm only one vote. I realize, this is a stretch. But one day, mark my words, it will happen.

Defrosting

Elizabeth Kirkpatrick-Vrenios

As I open the refrigerator door
the fluorescent glare attacks me
the last month curled
and blown away leaving me startled

at the myriad of colors
proliferating on the glass shelf
jostling against each other
like bullies on a playground.

The cheddar is nude and stubbled,
cream coagulated and sour.
Are those fuzzy blue mounds
the peaches I put there only a few weeks ago?

I enter a battlefield
without the will to fight,
my resolve as soft as cheese.
Right now all I want is a poem

perhaps something about
human kindness
or changing leaves
or redbud growing.

But the dark leak
of melting ice
puddles urgently,
and begins to creep across the floor.

Thin Line

Elizabeth Kirkpatrick-Vrenios

I stare
at the edge
some call
the horizon
where water
and sky touch,

reduced to one line
an abstract
painting
where the sun
disappears
each day
to reveal
what was always
there
suddenly I swim   with the ravens   wings spread,

catch the breeze   that carries me
over the thin line
and I sense   in my shadowed flight
the vast canopy

and waiting with their lamps   the day-blind stars.

The House Up Little Lake Road

Elizabeth Kirkpatrick-Vrenios

Think about the sun
peeking through a shutter
still hanging by its hinge,
how light pushes
through the cracks
to reveal spider webs
in the cracked corners,
how breezes stroke
the overgrown wild mustard
like the touch
of a beloved's skin,
and the days roll over
the sagging roof
leaving remnants
of maple leaves
long fallen,
and glitter in the blue,
blue everywhere,
sky touching the ground
wrapping its arms around you
and your lungs fill
with the stillness
of everything fresh and wide,
and the small knocking
of the heart
reminds you
you are the first singing light,
the candle in the dusk,
you are the pulse
that keeps this house warm.

Cheers, a toast to the world

Elizabeth Kirkpatrick-Vrenios

as I would have it, not as it is.
To my past: may its cloak be warm,
my present: may I always break the rules,
my future: may it continue its tattoo against my window.
To light: may it always be playing with darkness along the wet sand.
To joy: may it emerge from under the bark of every hour.
To green: may it continue to uncurl and hold out its palm to spring.
To hyacinths: fragrant cake ornaments and silent bells,
children's laughter: all that's glass, song, fire and salt,
fairy tales: that tether me to the world.
Here's to adoration: may it ever be squandered on the humble,
to plot: this small thread that roots my life,
music: a curl of daybreak and stillness.
To grief: an orchard I know.
To endurance: that's the word, I think.

CRITICISM

Megan Nolan's *Ordinary Human Failings*: A Study in the Relationship Between Denial and Mediocrity

Genna Rivieccio

In Megan Nolan's debut novel, *Acts of Desperation*, she was already setting her narrative in the "past." Even if the period of time she focuses on (2012, ultimately ending in 2019) still doesn't feel all that remote to many. With her second offering, *Ordinary Human Failings*, Nolan takes the time period even further back. Specifically, to 1990... with additional flashbacks to the seventies that also provide glimpses into Carmel Green's life before "the fall."

Like the nameless narrator in *Acts of Desperation*, Carmel is also an "anti-heroine" in that she doesn't fit neatly, by any stretch of the imagination, into a "good girl" categorization. Though she might have been able to were it not for succumbing to most women's mental health demise: love. More to the point, loving an older boy named Derek when she was a young, impressionable teenage girl. Worse still, naïve enough to believe in certain things as a result of that youth—like "happily ever after."

Inspired in part by Gordon Burn's 1984 nonfiction book, *Somebody's Husband, Somebody's Son: The Story of the Yorkshire Ripper*, Nolan read in said work that a journalist tried to tempt Peter Sutcliffe's family to give him tidbits and stories—in short, "an exclusive"—about Peter in exchange for putting them up in a hotel and supplying them with

> "Carmel...decided to deny her daughter's existence in every way possible from the moment she realized this 'creature' was growing inside her. Because it was from that moment forward that Carmel understood her life to be 'over,' her potential wasted. Just another ordinary human failing, as it were. To be sure, the title smacks of Chekhovian resignation, with the following *Three Sisters* quote coming to mind: 'Why is it, that when we've just started to live, we grow dull, gray, uninteresting, lazy, useless, with flattened-out souls?'"

seemingly limitless supplies of alcohol. Preying on the weakness of their working-class station in life and propensity for alcoholism, it got Nolan's wheels turning about two of her favorite subjects: classism in Britain and "the family." Per Nolan, "I started to imagine another crime that could bring about that situation." (Not to mention a viable time period during which tabloids had bigger budgets to facilitate such a situation.) And the crime she imagined is one of the most heinous variety: a child committing murder against another, even younger child. Indeed, it is none other than Carmel's ten-year-old daughter, Lucy, who is accused of killing a three-year-old girl named Mia Enright that lives in the same council estate as the Green family. A family that has been recently diminished after losing its matriarch, Rose, also acting as Lucy's mother figure in lieu of Carmel, who decided long ago to deny her daughter's existence in every way possible from the moment she realized this "creature" was growing inside of her. Because it was from that moment forward that Carmel understood her life to be "over," her potential wasted. Just another ordinary human failing, as it were. To be sure, the title smacks of Chekhovian resignation, with the following *Three Sisters* quote coming to mind: "Why is it, that when we've just started to live, we grow dull, gray, uninteresting, lazy, useless, with flattened-out souls?"

This, in effect, is what happens to Carmel once she not only discovers she's pregnant, but that Derek is planning to move to Dublin, with no intention of asking her to come along. It is soon after this revelation that she kicks into "Peggy Olson from *Mad Men*" mode, totally denying the extremely overt state of her expanding body. As the weeks—then months—start to pass, she begins to rely on wearing baggy clothes and/or belting down her stomach to hide the reality that she herself can't acknowledge, let alone declare to anyone else. It would be too much to speak aloud this simultatneous shame and *failure*.

As for the term "ordinary human failings," it comes up more than once in the book, but the first time is at the office where tabloid journalist Tom Hargreaves works. It is one of his fellow amoral coworkers, Edward, that wields the phrase by sending out a memo (back when that word was more universally understood) that reads: "Reasonable excuses [for lateness/missing meetings/not doing something] do NOT INCLUDE ordinary human failings such as hangovers, broken hearts, etc etc etc." Though it is aimed at the journalists, Nolan is making an obvious dig at Carmel and the rest of her family (save, perhaps, for Rose), who have so blatantly let their ordinary human failings become an excuse for indulging in even more *extra*ordinary ones.

In Carmel's case, the most extraordinary is her total failure as a mother, not bothering at all to look after Lucy in anything beyond the most cursory of ways. As such, Lucy is shown even less attention and affection after Rose's death. Accordingly, it doesn't take a shrink to assess that some of her increased acting out extends to her odd "playing" behavior with Mia and a few of the other kids. Granted, no one knows for sure if Lucy was really the responsible party for the child's death, with police taking her in for questioning just as Tom gets what he believes to be the first scoop on the story thanks to the dumb luck of going out on a date with a girl who also lives in the same council flats.

With his "insider" perspective, it doesn't take Tom long to paint a lurid depiction of Lucy and the Greens, with an article that says, among other things, "The family of this beloved little girl, her neighbors, the people of London and the people of Britain—all of us deserve to feel safe and to know that the subhuman creature who did this can't hurt any more children, will be swiftly apprehended and will pay dearly for what they have done." While the Enrights, Etta and Charles, are depicted as saintly humans, the Greens are, as expected, left to play the part of dastardly villains, further compounded by the fact that they're Irish immigrants. Undoubtedly a "sect of humanity" that Tom and Edward would bill as "peasants" the way they do practically everybody else. As the narrator puts it, "Peasants, that was what Edward and the others... called everyone who was not a journalist or royalty or a celebrity. Peasants were the cheapo hookers who'd had it off with footballers getting paid a few hundred quid for a tell-all, peasants were single mothers with hyperactive children who they could sell as NEIGHBORS FROM HELL... Peasants were crooks, bin men whining over wages, alcoholics, churchgoing Holy Joes, old people ringing in complaining about telly storylines, but most importantly, most of all, peasants were the readers."

And yet, the Greens are hardly of the demographic that reads tabloids, even if they still fall into Tom and Edward's "peasant" classification for other reasons. But it doesn't take Tom very long—after cajoling them all into the hotel where the booze will be free-flowing (music to Richie and John's [Carmel's brother and father, respectively] ears)—to come to the conclusion that Carmel is "special." Or rather, she had all the conditions early on in life to become properly special at her current age. It's just that things went horribly askew the instant her legs did for Derek. After which it is without any reservations that Carmel blames the unwanted trajectory of *her* existence on *Lucy's* existence. Something Carmel didn't even have the chance to stop in time because she waited too long for her secret to be outed. When Rose did finally catch sight of her daughter's uncovered belly, Carmel was too many months along to get an abortion—as she was scoldingly told at a London clinic where, as usual, the judgment was tenfold because of Carmel's Irishness.

Thus, although she may have technically resigned herself to this new and unwanted life of mediocrity, her more overpowering resolve to enter a state of denial is what, in her mind, spares her from totally forgoing the superior life she might have had were it not for the birth of Lucy.

At the beginning of the novel, the narrator describes, "When

[Carmel] let herself pore over memories, she was hawkish. Filled with greed for one of the only pleasures remaining to her, raking through lost evenings and moments. It was rare that she did allow herself this. It had been so long that she knew there could only be a handful more times. It would not always be possible to summon precisely the fast-fading textures and tastes." One aspect of that inability to summon these memories more readily is also rooted in Carmel's perpetual state of denial, which asks the mind to negate everything tied to a specific source of trauma—in this instance, Lucy. So it is that it becomes more difficult to recall the "textures and tastes" of Derek, the boy she thought she would love (and who would love her back) forever. Or even Waterford, where the Greens originally hail from (as does Nolan herself).

In fact, it often seems as though forgetting everything about their past—no matter how detrimental it is to their present—is essential to Carmel, Richie and John's self-preservation. With each of them seeking to outrun a part of their personal history so unpleasant that they choose to dissociate from it entirely (Richie and John assuring that dissociation through the numbing agent of alcohol). Such a "coping mechanism," while supposedly helpful (in the short run, anyway) to this trio of would-be caretakers, leaves Lucy inherently isolated and ostracized amid her pack of wounded, emotionally stunted animals.

To that point, talking to/trusting no one is the Green family's modus operandi for so-called survival. Because the only thing worse than trying to rely on each other is letting in any outsiders who would simply "never understand." Hence, despite technically "starting over again" in London after Carmel is forced to have her baby (with Rose suggesting the move to avoid the inevitable small-town ridicule), no one ever bothers with "reinvention." Instead sequestering from the outside world as much as possible. Which highlights something Tom thinks about those who tell lies for their own unique ends: "This was something he would never get used to; how, so often, people believed what you told them for no other reason than the fact you had said it."

The Greens perhaps never bother telling anyone in London something to the contrary about who they were in Ireland because they know, at their core, they cannot erase the mediocre people they became there. Or escape the ordinary human failings that have followed them to their new city, de facto "new life." Alas, a new life can never come to fruition when one suffers from "wherever you go, there you are" syndrome. Or, worse still, wherever you go, there's the very real, unavoidable result of your teenage folly, thereby making denial a more herculean and self-harming effort than usual.

If you like The Opiate magazine, you'll love The Opiate Books. Find our current roster of titles (featured below) online or at your favorite bookstore. Visit theopiatebooks.com for more information.

Brontosaurus Illustrated
by Leanne Grabel
Released: June 2022
List price: $34.99

Megalodon
by Donna Dallas
Released: April 2023
List price: $10.99

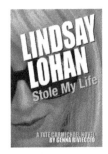

Lindsay Lohan Stole My Life
(A Tate Carmichael Novel)
by Genna Rivieccio
Released: April 2023
List price: $18.99

Yet So As By Fire: A Passion Play in Two Acts
by Anton Bonnici
Released: December 2021
List price: $12.99

Quasar Love: A Reenactment in Three Acts
by Anton Bonnici
Released: August 2022
List price: $12.99

Pornotopia: The Incomplete Texts
by Anton Bonnici
Released: July 2024
List price: $12.99

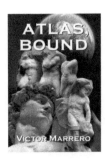

Atlas, Bound
by Victor Marrero
Released: July 2023
List price: $15.99

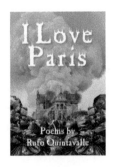

I Love Paris
by Rufo Quintavalle
Released: September 2023
List price: $10.99

This Rescue Thing
by Penny Allen
Released: April 2024
List price: $18.99

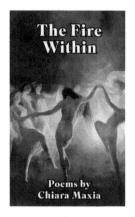

The PornME Trinity
(2nd Edition)
by David Leo Rice
Released: October 2022
List price: $12.99

On the Way to Invisible
by Antonia Alexandra Klimenko
Released: June 2024
List price: $14.99

The Fire Within
by Chiara Maxia
Released: September 2024
List price: $14.99

128.

Printed in the USA
CPSIA information can be obtained
at www.ICGtesting.com
LVHW052044021124
795422LV00021B/490